THE CANONGATE PRIZE
FOR NEW WRITING

Original Sins

THE CANONGATE PRIZE
FOR NEW WRITING

Original Sins

Canongate Books
IN ASSOCIATION WITH

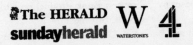

First published in Great Britain in 2001 by
Canongate Books Ltd, 14 High Street,
Edinburgh EH1 1TE

10 9 8 7 6 5 4 3 2 1

The publishers acknowledge subsidy from the
Scottish Arts Council towards the publication
of this volume

**For further information about the Canongate Prize for
New Writing, and details of how to enter next year's
competition, please visit:
www.canongateprize.com**

British Library Cataloguing-in-Publication Data
A catalogue record for this book is available
on request from the British Library

ISBN 1 84195 081 5

Typeset by Palimpsest Book Production Ltd,
Polmont, Stirlingshire
Printed and bound by Omnia Books Ltd, Glasgow

Contents

Foreword

What is sin, anyway? It's a word that's bandied about a lot, usually with reference to something that gives us particular pleasure. I've seen chocolate confections on restaurant menus that were described as 'so good they are positively sinful'. Macaulay said the Puritans opposed bear-baiting not because it gave pain to the bears, but because it gave pleasure to the onlookers. So what's wrong with pleasure? The old-fashioned religious answer was that it might endanger your eternal soul. The thinking was that this life was not the real thing; it was only a preparation for the true life that lay beyond death. There's an old hymn that captures it perfectly:

> *Brief life is here our portion,*
> *Brief sorrow, short lived care;*
> *The life that knows no ending,*
> *The tearless life, is there.*
>
> *O happy retribution,*
> *Short toil, eternal rest,*
> *For mortals and for sinners*
> *A mansion with the blest.*

*   *   *

That's not exactly laugh-a-minute stuff, but there is a certain logic in it, if you buy the basic premise. If the real life lies Beyond, and if this life is a test that fixes forever where you end up after death, then you are going to have to be very careful about what you get up to down here. Inevitably, that way of thinking leads to enormous anxiety, so questions about what's allowed and what's absolutely forbidden become very important. That's why the old religious codes on the subject were unbelievably detailed. Priests used to be given manuals that worked out the exact sin content in any particular sexual act, for instance. The basic premise was that sex itself was problematic. Since the Fall in the Garden of Eden it had become the means whereby sin and guilt were passed on to the frail children of Adam and Eve, so it had to be handled with extreme care. It was all right for the purposes of procreation within carefully licensed relationships, but apart from that, forget about it. The trouble was, of course, that it was impossible to forget about it, hence the need for all that detailed guidance. What about nocturnal emissions, for instance? It was acknowledged that wet dreams were involuntary, but they were useless as far as procreation went and they did give pleasure, so were they sinful? Well, the book said, they were OK if you stayed asleep throughout, but if you woke up and enjoyed it, then you were in trouble.

Laughable nonsense? If you are a happy, hedonistic post-religious person, then you'll probably think so. But if the contributions to Canongate's competition for the best writing on sin are anything to go by, then there is still a lot of angst about sin out there. And much of it is about sex. A certain kind of religious upbringing still seems to be productive of enormous pain and anger about human sexuality. Obviously, if you are a kid who thinks he might be gay and you belong to a religion that condemns homosexuality as a grave disorder, then you are going to be in big trouble inside your own head and heart. There were a number of entries that exposed that particular kind of pain. In fact, the thing that depressed me most about the competition was not the standard of the entries, which was extremely high, but the evidence they afforded that religion seems to be more productive of guilt than of goodness.

The trouble with sin lies precisely here: it is a negative concept; it tells us the kind of actions we should avoid, rather than the kind of people we should positively try to become. Given our human nature and its compulsions, we probably need both negative and positive versions of behaviour. Unfortunately, religion tends to put more emphasis on the negative side, it likes telling us what not to do. The interesting thing to note here is that it is theoretically possible to obey all the negative commandments and totally ignore the positive ones; to keep out of trouble and never make a mistake, but never do anything really positive and good, never really love humanity. The difference lies in the motivation. If you are motivated by fear and obedience you will probably manage to keep your record clean and never get points on your licence to live; but you probably won't put much back into life, won't make much difference for the better to any other human being. On the other hand, if your motive is positive not negative, if you act from love rather than obedience, then you will probably make an enormous difference in actual people's lives. You may technically be what the Church thinks of as a sinner, someone who's broken the commandments, but you may also be someone who has loved people, someone who has been more interested in helping others than in keeping yourself out of trouble. I think that's the better way to live. Better a loving sinner than an unloving saint. Unfortunately, virtue is rarely exciting to read about, whereas sin is always a hot topic. That's why this is such an exciting book. Would there have been a book at all, if the topic had been virtue?

Richard Holloway

ORIGINAL SINS

THE CANONGATE PRIZE
FOR NEW WRITING

Original Sins

KEVIN BROOKS
Goodnight

A midday pub in Waterloo, hungover black hat and glasses and a dirty black suit. Jukebox Madonna and beer-wet tables and red velveteen benchseats, the bar is crowded with loud magazine and TV people in creased jeans and short jackets or work-crumpled skirts, and a video screen on the wall shows models on a catwalk.

Cigarette smoke drifts in the hubbub, I think of God in a grubby grey dress, walking on the ceiling. I think I've had enough of this. The magazine man is buying more drinks at the bar, the long-haired photographer went to the toilet twenty minutes ago and now I see him by the cigarette-machine laughing with a bull-headed man in a waistcoat and collarless shirt.

I light another cigarette.

Nick says *one* interview, for me, Paul, just one, for Christ's sake. We're going down the pan.

All right.

This is it, half-cooked.

His name is Chris something, he wrote a book, so he tells me. Red hair like a red dog, high head, long fingers, eyes always five minutes on. He wears a russet jacket with a small enamel badge pinned to the lapel, a loose white shirt and pointy shoes. Walks like a goose. Here he comes, drinks on a bent tray, sideways grin and a hack's wink at someone over by the door. Rock'n'roll man. He does it well, but I imagine him at home at night with black coffee and gum and a gonk on his desk, working hard at the keyboard, working hard at it.

'There you go,' he says – one, two, three, four – looks around and leans the empty tray against the wall, sups his lager and sits. Dr Feelgood pumping on the jukebox now, 'Down at the Doctor'. A glass breaks behind the bar, a brief lull and then muted cheers. I position my drinks in front of me like a punchy chessman. One, two, three. Check. I asked for three just to see what happened.

'So,' he breezes, clacking a fresh tape into his mini-recorder, 'what are you—'

'Excuse me, I'll be back in a minute.'

In the toilets there's a man with a goatee hawking into a sink. I find a cubicle with a lock and empty myself of whisky piss and shovel a thumbful of speed up my nose. Sit down. Listen, shoes scuffing on tiles, ochre hiss, pipes, coughs, farts, the muffled ring of alcohol and the beep of tills. We're going down the pan. It's not hard to leave without being seen. I'll ring him later. No, I won't.

Along the wide Thames it's cold and drizzle-grey. An empty pleasure boat chops in the gloom, green and white canopy flapping in the wind and bits of stick and fish and feathers lap against the river wall. Polystyrene fish. Knock knock. I don't know where I am but it's not too far from anywhere. Station, arches, towers, statues, bridges, roads, kiosks, bits of park, galleries and steps and sketchpad students, a coachload of Japanese teddy boys and teddy girls limp-quiffed and forlorn in the London rain. Hot dogs. Plastic hats. Newspapers. Winter lights of cars and taxis and suits and umbrellas and scaffolds and generators and the smell of cheap perfume like sweets in a bag and tight jumpers and legs and watching out for nothing you walk like a lion in your cold sweated suit and hat with your scarecrow hair itching in the subway steam and glue-eyed beggars spit and gasp and subterranean shriek, it's a small world under the fluorescent skies tonight.

In a long Piccadilly tunnel you squat down against the tiled wall to stem the swirl and drink from your bottle. The heat of the underground streams past, a thousand clacking legs and feet flowing round you like flotsam circumnavigating a drowned dog.

Surface tension.

Traffic accident.

Repulsion.

Red eyes on the level, a gangly Irish youth with brown teeth and a twisted gob.

'Hey.'

You look at him, crouched in front of you.

'Where's the score?' he says.

'What?'

'You're using, John. Where is it?'

When you don't answer he blinks stiffly and lifts a used-up hand towards your face. You see a black tattoo scab on his wrist, then crack him in the head with the whisky bottle.

*   *   *

Later, in the evening dark – what comes of this? Like a childhood episode told too many times the memory of this day has taken on the distance of another's tale. I have no idea of my truth. No matter – leaving the Yorkshire Grey around six, two *guys* are coming in, drunk as hell, asking me where the action is. One of them a very ugly-looking olive thing, breathing sweet breath in my face, the other wearing sheer baggy trousers that billow in the wind and cling to the shape of his groin. I say nothing and walk out into the stale air, feeling lousy. I want something, I don't know what. I don't want anything. Centre Point sticks up white and grey in the night, checkerboard windows here and there looking down at the middle of the world. Buses, shops, theatre, subway. Kiosk. Railings on the corner for leaning on. Roast-chestnut man. Down Oxford Street, I hate this street of slouch and fucking tat. Why don't you go home? Because. I don't know. I'm looking for the devil. Jesus. Top Man, perfumery on a brickboard, shoppers in soft coats in the cold wind, new clothes and coffee pots in carrier-bags, so I turn down a Soho side street and graze the grilled windows of magazine places and skimpywear and Chinese knives. The drink keeps out the worst of the cold. But still. Is it too late for you?

In a step-down doorway a flimsy sign says Young Blonde, with a line drawing of a bow-lipped girl in a skintight costume. High corridor and narrow stairs with wooden railings, dim and dun (like *Barbary Shore*), and before I know it (I know it) I'm down through the doorway onto the hard-floor corridor and smelling the scattered dust. Along the hallway a man appears behind a hatchway door. Tall and muscled light-skinned black in a bronze-black T-shirt, chewing on a stick of liquorice. I didn't know—

'Yeah?'

'The—'

'See the girl?'

'How do you mean?'

He sucks his teeth. 'You looking for the girl?'

'The one on the sign?'

'She on the sign. How 'bout it?'

I look around, how did I get here? Look up the stairs, see nothing but a bedsit world of thick paint and dull risers in a paper shade light. Nothing, but something there leads me on, sets my heart.

'Hey, chief,' the pimp says, 'this ain't no peep show.'

'Right.'

'Fifty a throw, hunnerd the night.' He looks at his wrist-watch. 'Till midnight. Fifty a throw, hunnerd till midnight.'

'The girl on the sign?'

'Yeah, don' worry 'bout it.'

'Okay.'

Chewing, staring at me. 'Okay *what*?'

I take a fifty from my pocket and pass it over. He snaps the note and folds it into his pocket, says, 'First floor, second door on the right. Name's Cindy. Damage the goods I take it out your neck.' He smiles, liquoriced teeth. 'Enjoy yourself.'

Then he's gone.

Halfway up the stairs my legs turn to rope. Something smells bad and I think it's me. Unwashed, whisky and dirty wet streets, I smell and feel like a wanker. So what? So what, in the silence of bare carpet and draped windows, so what? I'm a wonderful man. I haven't done anything. (And, remember, I have no idea if this *is* my truth. For all I know, for all I know I'm making it up, dredging up the bones of another story, moulding them to my own. Why would I do that? To impress you? Why not? To *impress* you.) So what?

The door is spunk-white and scuffed at the base through kicking where it jams. Just as I'm pausing to ponder the etiquette of a prostitute's door (knock? walk in? call out?) it opens with a rattle and a practised tug and there she is, none too steady in heels and a fuck-green dress and bottled hair. Young as you like, old as you like. Drugslim, potbelly tight in satin, skewed jaw and green my eyes.

'How do you do?' I say.

She cracks a one-sided smile and opens the door. I walk in, she kicks it shut, goes across to a bedside table and lifts a burning cigarette from an ashtray, sits sideways on the edge of the bed jiggling her foot up and down, smoking, watching me. I don't know what to do. It's a small room. Bed, wardrobe, white rug on the floor. Two-bar electric fire. A beaded curtain hangs in a doorway to a bathroom. Soft red light glows from a cylindrical lamp beside the bed. Look at the girl. See what you like.

'Cindy?' I say.

She shrugs, taps a tube of cigarette ash into the ashtray and smooths her dress. 'You ready?'

'What?'

The cigarette is balanced on the rim of the ashtray, then she stands up and pulls the dress over her head. That smile again, in shineless skin and catalogue underwear, a grazed elbow and puckered appendix scar, a body.

'Is that your real name?'

'Say what?'

'Cindy. Is it your real name?'

'Yeah, let's go.'

'Just a minute.'

'What, just a minute?'

'Have you got anything to drink? I need a drink.'

She looks at me, idly scornful, reaches for her cigarette. 'You want a waitress, too?'

I don't know what she means. 'I'm happy to pay.'

She laughs, coughing out a stream of smoke, then stoops to fetch a bottle of Smirnoff from beneath the bedside table. As she bends I study her backside, a tight stretch of black lace, a thumbed bruise high on her thigh. I hear the clink of bottle on glass, see her sneak a drink from the bottle, screw the cap back on, set it down carefully on the floor. See on the wall above her a small wooden Jesus on a cross and dried flowers in a wall vase and a *Giant Puzzler* magazine on the table. I see it all in black and white, like a dated TV documentary. When she turns and hands me two inches of vodka in a dusty tumbler the whore smile is gone, replaced by a worn out grin.

'On the house,' she says, watching me drink it down.

'Thank you.'

She takes the empty glass and puts it on the table, turns again to face me with breasts and mocking eyes. 'Well?'

'Do you want to talk for a while?'

'What about?'

'I don't know. Anything.'

'What's the matter?'

'Nothing. I just thought you might want to talk . . .'

She lights a fresh cigarette and sits down on the bed, hitching a bra strap. 'Go on then.'

'What?'

'If you're going to talk, talk. You got about ten minutes.'

I can't think of anything to say. I could ask her how she comes to be in this place, sitting around in her underwear, fucking people, but I doubt she'd tell me. So I light a cigarette and ask her where she's from.

'Nowhere,' she says. Getting up, she finds a hanger for her dress, hangs it in the doorway, sits down again.

'Do you live here?'

'You what?'

'What do you do? During the day, I mean.'

'Fuck.'

'But when you're not . . . what do you like to do?'

She shrugs. 'Nothing much. Sleep, watch TV.' A yawn. 'Look, I got things to do. Do you want it or not?'

For a moment I know I'm not here, I never was, this is someone else's day – *dialogue between opponents* – *dispersal* – *cultivation in a wilderness* – *incision* – *pause for a breather* – *rise and fall* – *hello again, sweetmeat* – and I know what I'm supposed to say.

I say, 'No, I'm sorry. I shouldn't be here. I don't feel right. Do you mind if we don't?'

She comes on to me, interested. 'What's the matter?'

'Nothing, really.' (How does it go?) 'I had an operation recently.'

'Yeah?'

'A craniotomy.'

'A what?'

'In my head, just here.' I touch a hand to the side of my head. 'I'm still recuperating.' She rises on tiptoe to peer closely at my head, brushing herself against me. I step back a little. 'I'd better go.'

'You know,' she says, 'you look familiar, like someone off the TV. Lemme think.'

She's standing there as good as naked, hand on hip, smoking her cigarette, looking me up and down, and now I know who she is and what's going to happen.

Her name is Sunny.

She clicks her fingers. 'The one off the music show, that's it. You look like him – what's his name?'

'I don't know.'

'Yeah, you do. A couple of years ago, on ITV. There was him and that girl off the quiz show, with the Scotch guy. You know?'

'No, I don't.'

Then she smiles and puts her hand between my legs.

I move away. 'I'm sorry, no, I can't . . . my head.'

She looks at me like I stink of shit. 'Listen,' she says, 'you think I like doing this? What do you—'

'I paid, didn't I?'

'Paid that cunt downstairs.'

'I'm sorry.'

'What do you wanna come here for if you can't fuck, innit? What's the matter with you?'

'I thought I was all right.'

'Yeah?'

'Look, let me give you something for the drink.' I take a twenty from my pocket and hand it over, tell her thanks.

'What's this?'

'For your inconvenience.'

'This is twenty. It's fifty.'

'No, I already paid. Like you said, I paid the man downstairs.'

'Fifty,' she says.

'I paid fifty, you know it. That's all you're going to get.'

'Yeah?' Dirty and cold, she turns her back, goes to the doorway to fetch her dress. Puts it on. Young as you like, old as you like. Drugslim, potbelly tight in satin, skewed jaw and green my eyes.

'Fuck off,' she says.

Now we both know what it is.

On the way out I'm fearful she's called the pimp and told him something, I hit her or something, and I stop on the stairs to light a cigarette like that's going to scare him to death. He sees me smoking a cigarette, he'll think I'm hard as fucking nails, best leave me alone, innit? But nothing happens, there's no one around. I walk out into the Soho drizzle and head for the tube station and home.

If it didn't happen, I don't know what did.

But this is it. The lights are out when I get back. Off-licence whisky heavy in my pocket, wet gate, gate-posts, wet leaves on the path. November moon in a raked black sky, fireworks. Dogs barking at the whistles and screes and booms and the crackle and smell of garden bonfires across the street. The

Peugeot sits rained and gold in the driveway and stuck with leaves, in the way, fucking thing, kick it, sorry. Remember Chris – the magazine man – remember him? I wonder if he snarled. Searching for my keys, in the same pocket as the whisky bottle so I have to yank it out, rip the pocket. The front door opens to a cold house. 'Nicola!'

I don't usually call out, and maybe I don't, I don't know. I think I do. I remember wondering why I'm doing it, and then surprised at the tension in my voice. You know when a house is empty, the air tells you. This house isn't empty, but it's cold and dark and something isn't right. God knows what. I'm about as drunk as I can get but I'm used to it. In this state I function admirably. So I drop my keys and stuff on the hall table and go around turning on lights and fires, checking this and that, a cigarette, a swig from the bottle, not calling out now, just taking it easy. Taking it easy. Heart bursting in lead. Outside the fireworks are cracking away – *sheeee, zip, k k k k ka ka ka, booomshhhh* . . . every downstairs light is on, put all the lights on, put them all on, make everything all right. Up the stairs, you have to go up the stairs, swinging the bottle in your hand. One, two, three . . . a sickle of silver studs in her ear. One, two, three . . . her eyelids flicker. One, two, three . . . this way. Through the arch, see the rocking horse? Nicola's. Upstairs. One, two, three . . . pause on the third step to say goodnight, didn't you always? Lucky, lucky, lucky. Mum and Dad in the front room, barley wine and cigarettes and late night TV, shut the door, into the hallway, up the stairs – fieldfares and wheatears and a kingfisher on the wall – pause on the third step to say goodnight, and don't you dare start climbing again until you hear them say it back.

Goodnight. Say it again if you have to – goodnight – because if you move before they reply – God help us – it's monsters all round. And don't say you don't believe it. One, two, three . . . wait. Goodnight. One, two, three, four, five, six, seven, eight and here we are. Take my hand. This way, let me show you something. The lights are on. Up to the top of the stairs to the top of the stairs, to pause for a drink to stem the weird comfort and you say and you say and you say, I'm a sick and nasty little girl. No. Along the landing, ignoring the bedroom doors, you know where you're going, you can see it all along. I know where I'm going, I can see it all along. Here the world hums in my head as I open the bathroom door, and there she lies always, bled white and cold in the bath. You look at her, please. See how beautiful she is, even now, with her wrists hacked open and her bloodless frame wrinkled limp in pink water. Oh, Nicola. How clean and determined you are. A smeared red handprint on the side of the bath the only hint of doubt, and even that – after I've sat crying with you for the rest of the night – even that I know to be nothing more than an adjustment, a move to comfort. See the note? See the hand? Read it, please. *All the noise and stupidity in my head is gone.* That's it, your essence of every dead day. Your torment, your purity, your bride.

That's it.

JENNIFER CLEMENT

A Salamander-Child

1

My mother is my aunt. My father is my uncle. My name is Elizabeth Medora Leigh, but everyone calls me Elizabeth, which means 'Consecrated by God'. I was conceived in the 'Year of the Great Frost'.

My mother explained what happened to her like this: 'With a face of veils and dusk, I lived scorned and apple-full, because my brother drew the lines inside my hands and birthmarked me for him. "Bird" and "dearest of all", he called me. I was his half-sister, half-heart, the wish-half of the wishbone.'

My mother said she couldn't escape. That it was like trying to stop breathing, or blinking, or being warm and that time became only the time for closing doors. But the great hive of moon followed them inside, even the stars broke into their rooms, they had to search for shadows, for the night and forest, needing the full, blind black so he could say, in drunken voice, all bear-heavy and slow, 'This is a dream, Augusta.' Each and every morning he'd leave her sad slumber, unlock his hands from hands so like his own, vowing to drink her out of himself and to forget her face of dark worship. But later in the morning-room, at church, at tea, and through all the crowds he'd stare at her as if his eyes alone could steal her warm, round breath, still quivering with the beat of her heart, that fell along her arms.

At first they were frightened. What grew inside my mother? No one said a word, but in their quiet thoughts they imagined a child with goat hooves for feet. A child who could count to five, but with six fingers on each hand. A child with three livers and without a spleen. A salamander-child. My mother said she prayed on stones, blackened her cheeks with soot, and wept with a sound like ripped cloth, frightened birds and shovels breaking earth. She became hymn-filled and full of promises: 'I promised God I'd never play cards again. I promised God I'd never miss church again. I promised God I'd never touch him again.'

My father said, 'If the child's an ape so be it. It is my fault alone!'

Touching his arm was touching her own arm. Kissing him was kissing her own lips. The scent of his hair was the scent of her own locks. The taste of his saliva was the taste of her own blood. She missed him when he was with her like wanting the ocean when she was in the sea or wanting sugar when she was sucking on an orange, or wanting daybreak at noon. When she spoke he knew what she would say.

She said, 'Yes.'

2

I was born at Six Mile Bottom on April 15th 1814 and christened there, May 20th 1814 by the Reverend C. Wedge. My mother placed all her mirrors into drawers and cupboards. I had no caul. I did not have a club foot. I had the mixed blood of brother and sister, which is the colour of milk, white because it contains too much salt. I was born of a crime for which there is no salvation in this world.

My mother said, 'She smells of what I imagine lilies smell like – without a smell – the scent of green stalk.'

My aunt said, 'She looks just like me.'

My father said, 'She came from the Euphrates River, or from the Nile.'

My uncle said, 'Show me her feet! They are the feet I should have had.'

My mother said, 'Her eyes are just like mine, but even darker.'

My father said, 'Her eyes are just like mine, but even darker.'

My aunt said, 'Her eyes are just like mine, but even darker.'

*   *   *

My uncle said, 'Her eyes are just like mine, but even darker.'

Nothing could protect me or give me shelter. Nothing would stand between my body and the wolf. For twelve years my mother brushed my hair, bought me dresses, cleaned my teeth and face, saying, 'It is my face too. You belong to me.'

Everyone knew. Everyone looked at me too closely. Everyone stared at Lord Byron's child, a child of sin, a child of incest and adultery, a child no man should ever touch – half human and half animal.

There were no faceless informers, no witnesses, no interrogation. Instead, my father wrote and published the poems that damned them. He wrote:

> *I speak not, I trace not, I breathe not thy name,*
> *There is grief in the sound, there is guilt in the frame;*
> *But the tear which now burns on my cheek may impart*
> *The deep thoughts that swell in that silence of heart.*

This was written so I would not hear a sound.

3

Every day I come down the stairs of the house with an overcast face, a Byron-face, barren mouth, hair like a bratt covering my head. In the glade of my neck there is heat. I say my house has clean water. This is what I call myself: Elizabeth. My name means 'Consecrated by God', and not

'Wise Counsellor', 'Gazelle', or 'Branch'. I hold open hand to show I am not carrying a weapon. These are all the things I have thought about:

My face is faceless, a sea that wants to be the ocean. How light my body feels, how sure I am that my arms can carry me. I count my fingers that taste like grass: this happens to those without shelter. My body heat is still inside the sweater's sleeves, the phantom body of legs and hips in the skirt are folded over a chair. These clothes where I belong protect my skin from wind and sun and skin of others. My dresses want to move and cross their arms, lift themselves up, walk.

Yesterday, beneath the bluff, a dead man was found. His jack-o'-lantern face cracked open, skull with small hole dipped into by bird. He lay with flint arrows and one spear. Where once he tasted the blue pine, they pulled him out and found the secret tattoos: blue cross behind his knee, blue flower inked on ankle. There, in his smallest piece of flesh, were the shapes of ant hills, hives of molecules, colours of bluebottle flies, the sounds of summer. I studied his hands, his ribs, and seams. The bones of his spine lay on the ground like a ladder. I wanted to walk along those bleached stepping-stones. I thought he was my cousin.

Today along the water spine of the river there are so many broken glass bottles the shallow waves chime. I close my eyes because it will be as if I am not here. The sea travels in my blood and wants to be the ocean. I've thought of this before. I build a steeple with my hands.

*   *   *

I know the rabbit meat is under-cooked. The potatoes are green, the plum jelly is too black. I have tried some remedies since prayer is not enough. I have seen my face in someone's eyes. No one has ever said, 'There, there . . .'

. . . It is a dim and thistled dawn, too silent for rising. Two dresses stand in my room on poles. Two pairs of shoes by my bed. In the very last prune-dark minutes – where no bird sound breaks – can feel the light returning to the stars.

It is too quiet yet for prayers.

I remember when they slit the deer's belly and the foetus lay furless but with small hooves formed, 'Counts as two! This is a good omen.' The hunters clapped their hands, bit their thumbs and slapped their thighs. One man said to his son, 'Don't whine, boy, be a man, be a prince. The hunt was ripe!'

No one will place their body between my body and the bear.

The seamstress measures my waist: 22 inches. Measures inches around thigh and wrist. Length of neck: 5 inches. Weight: 9 stone. Cobblers measure my feet. Left: 6 inches. Right: 5 inches.

My mother once told me, 'Your first breath, birth-breath, smelled like the river and dry grass.' I cup hands around my mouth to smell the 16-year-old breath of river, dry grass, milk.

Smell of acorn and wool, smell of mother and father. There are the shapes of people in the air. A hand moves through bower and thistle, arms alter the swell along brick and tile, someone walks an orbit. See the cloud shaped like my dress, rain falls through the fold and lint. This minute while I am breathing a sailor blows out a candle. My father is in Greece. Some things I have seen. They were not asked for.

There is no pitter-patter in the breeze that blows the whisper of my father's voice through the air following my mother's words that are misshapen and mixed where alphabet becomes geography. Other words move around the house, into cups. I write in the air as I walk with the penmanship of my body.

My mother said his words blew in the air and into her blouse. She said she had a dream. In her dream dirt fell, and ash and gravel. A miscast rain.

4

This is not the house that Jack built, nor the crooked house with a crooked fence, this is the house of a wife, a cook, a mop and a pail. The house of whispers. Nailed to the wall, this is not a star but bent and brittle branches – the dry skeleton of a kite. This is not a swallow but a small clipped hawk step, step, stepping under the willow's shade. And this, this is not a goldfish but a black spotted salamander, gills against glass where there is no reef or stone.

Today my mother told me I have always known you and you

are what I have found. She said, before you were born you called to me for water. I do not deny God and my mouth has kissed my hand. Your father told everyone. He was not a gentleman. He did not know how to keep quiet.

My parents said they were so alike they cast one shadow.

My mother told me another dream. She was with a crowd of people who were saying she had arms for pushing wheelbarrows. She is a woman who never left the cave, or feared fire. She asked my father to drink her tears. She could poison him with her body. She says she is homesick when she's home. She misses the chair she sits in. She longs for the dress she is wearing. She says that the first time she saw my father she wanted to see him. The first time she touched his arm she wanted to touch his arm. She thought: I wish he were sick. I wish he had a fever so I could care for him. He is lame. He has to lean on me.

I know how to tie sheepshank rope knots, figure-eight knots, and bowline knots with my eyes closed. With my eyes closed I can knit, cook, and walk to the corner, and the cathedral. If I close my eyes no one see me. The chemist says I have night-blindness. I cannot see the nut-pick, nutcracker, pan or pail. I drink a fluidram of raisin water, a fluid ounce of prune water and wash my eyes with apple vinegar. If I could see, I would find my way.

My mother said that she had followed him for miles. She knew the sound of his footsteps, the twist and clap of his twisted boot on stone. She said she wanted to lie down so he could walk over her body. She said that this is what happened: A spirit lives in me in a place between the apple and the apple skin, a place between sleep and morning, between my skin and blood. He is black and white, polished and dangerous as a domino. The beat of his boots is in my voice, the blow of his boots is in my voice. Yoked to my waist, he whispers with a breath of hooves and wagon wheels. At daybreak, I comb tangle and snarl from my hair, wet my eyes, wash my eyes. Even though I knot my fingers, tie them together, he still holds my hands. She learned that inside or outside, it was still the same night.

5

Since I could find no love or someone to love me, I had to look for love close to my house. I loved, but I disliked, my half-sister's husband, Henry Trevanion. I broke my own sister's heart. Betrayed her in her own house and bed. Betrayed her as I drank her water and ate her cake. While my sister nursed his babies I nursed her husband at my breast. He followed me around the house pushing me up against walls and kissing me, placing his hand under my skirt at the dinner table. Touching his wife's sister again and again. He said I tasted sweeter, younger and better than my sister. I was fourteen. It was then my sister told me I was 'the result of adultery and incest'. I knew my face and knew she spoke the truth.

When everyone found out I was carrying Henry's child they

took me to a phrenologist who felt my head and told me the bumps of my skull showed a severe destructive tendency. A head, he said, with the shape of a salamander. I was placed in an asylum where the windows were nailed shut and the doors were bolted with chains. I lost that child. I lost several more.

* * *

Elizabeth Medora died on August 29th 1849 at four in the afternoon from smallpox. At this time she had been married for only one year to a Frenchman, Jean-Louis Taillefer, with whom she had a son, Elie, who died aged forty-four without heirs. Her daughter by Henry Trevanion, Marie, entered the convent in 1858 at the age of twenty-two where she took her vows and became Sister Sainte-Hilaire. In her Book of Hours she remembered her mother, drawing a memorial tombstone on which she inscribed 'Elizabeth Medora Byron' along with some lines by Lamartine (changing he to she):

> *Stretch over her thy pardoning hand.*
> *She sinned – but Heaven is a gift;*
> *She suffered – 'tis but innocence;*
> *She loved – 'tis the seal of forgiveness.*

NEIL COCKER

KGB Hairdressing

Today Kestas has found out that Brezhnev, in his all-seeing wisdom, has banned Pink Floyd's *Dark Side of the Moon*. This news makes him smile. He has a copy of the record hidden under his bed. He is now a criminal.

A trolley-bus clanks down the road, electric cable sparking and crackling. Vilnius old town is crumbling around him; the pastel coloured buildings are dirty and greying, wearing away with the years of ice and sooty fumes and the slow terminal gnawing of time. The street is scattered with people: old babushkas labouring to carry their sackcloth shopping bags, sweating under layers of waxy clothes; stocky, grizzled men with mottled and pitted faces, noses a thready explosion of vodka-burst veins; pretty girls in short skirts, their ice-blonde hair combed back into pony-tails. Nobody like him. Just as he is breathing the fresh spring air, tasting the lingering cold of winter in his lungs, two hands close on each of his arms, steely grips from behind.

He opens his mouth in surprise but his voice is knocked out of him by a hard nudge, jostling him forward, letting him sense their reckless strength. He keeps quiet. A quick glance to either side reveals two men, dressed the same in long thick coats and leather gloves. They say nothing and steer him down a side street. They stop at a pale brick building and push him through the door. The room is dark and quiet; as his eyes adjust, Kestas sees it is a Barber's shop. A small bald man in glasses stands by a mirror holding scissors. He looks worried and surprised, but there is a fear in his eyes that suggests he knows these men. They force Kestas down into a worn plastic chair in front of the mirror, and turn to the bald man. 'Cut.'

The bald man is overcome with a frightened energy. He scuttles around, comparing the blades of his scissors, moving from foot to foot and back again, muttering to himself. In the mirror, the two leather-gloved men are reflected. It is easy to look at them without their noticing. One has a dark, well-trimmed beard and is the taller of the two. The shorter man has a moustache and a squint nose. They both have an air of casual ruthlessness. KGB.

The barber comes forward and takes Kestas's long hair gently in his hands, pulling it loose onto his shoulders, untucking a few strands from his collar. He sighs almost inaudibly, a tiny breathless whine. Then he starts to cut. The scissors move quickly. Snick snick snick. Chunks of lank hair fall to the floor. In the mirror Kestas stares deep into his own eyes. When the barber is finished, he runs his rough hands over Kestas's bristling scalp, happy with his craftsmanship. With a shaving brush he dusts most of the hair off the shoulders of Kestas's denim jacket.

'Give me your papers.' The tall man is looking at him, staring into the mirror.

Kestas reaches inside his jacket. He takes out his wallet and removes his papers, folded twice. The tall man takes them from him. 'Kestas Kovalenko,' he says. The other man copies the name into a notebook. And probably his address too. Then the papers are returned to Kestas.

'You are something of a subversive. It is dangerous to have this look, this long hair. The American hippy. You will have to be careful, Comrade Kovalenko.'

The barber knocks something over and it clatters to the linoleum floor. Kestas catches a glimpse of himself in the mirror without meaning to and sees someone he doesn't recognise. The long hair has gone, cut to greasy brown stubble.

'You can go.' The tall man takes off his jacket. Kestas gets to his feet and squeezes past the two men. As he passes out the door into the street, he is blinded by harsh white sunlight. At the same moment a tuft of hair falls from a fold in his jacket and drifts to the ground like an autumn leaf.

*

He walks home from the factory, the Saturday shift finished, the familiar late afternoon relief. The relief feels different than usual though, because this last week everything has been confused and nothing feels normal anymore. Since the haircut he has developed a nervous habit, constantly running his hands over the top of his head. Again and again he does it, like he is stroking a dog.

In the last four days spring has finally overcome the winter. The ice in the air has gone. Every breath tastes of pollen and the fresh sweat of grass. The gentle sunshine has a flicker of warmth. But this stirs no feelings of joy in him; this may be a new beginning, the slow slide into summer, yet the truth is that after what happened in Vilnius it may be the beginning of the end.

Behind him he hears a car approaching, its sick engine grumbling. He steps onto the grassy bank, waiting for it to pass. But it slows down. He turns to see a white Lada with sprays of mud and patches of rust up the side. An elbow sticking out the window.

'Kestas!'

He squints through the reflection on the windscreen. 'Oh. Jonas.'

Jonas Vilkas is his cousin. He also works at the furniture factory, but is lazy, known as a layabout. There are rumours too that he has stolen chairs for the black market. The authorities have done nothing so far, but Kestas thinks it is only a matter of time.

'Kestas, where's your hair?'

'I got it cut. For summer.'

Jonas grins. He is the same age as Kestas, twenty-one. They grew up together, sat together in the English class at school, bored and swapping caricatures of their classmates when the teacher turned her back. But recently they have not been close. When Kestas's mother died, Jonas didn't even come to the funeral. And there is something else about Jonas too. The mocking smile he wears when he asks about Vaida and Erikas. The leer he wears when he sees Vaida, ogling her figure, making jokes about her teaching.

Jonas leans out of the window and passes him a bottle. Kestas examines it, full to the neck with clear liquid, no label. Samagonas; home made black bread vodka. As he tips the bottle back he closes his eyes. The breeze is quite warm and this affects the vodka. It tastes of summer: of long nights sitting with friends on the balcony, nibbling pink flesh from fish bones and sucking his sticky fingers. The samagonas burns its way down his throat. It is crisp and clean, pure and redeeming. He opens his eyes again. A small boy is passing on a bicycle, wheels whirring like some gangly, clumsy insect. 'It's good vodka.'

'The best. I make the best in Ukena.'

Kestas passes the bottle back to Jonas. He takes a slug, nods knowingly. 'You want to make some money, Kestas?'

'What're you talking about?'

'Get in the car. Let me tell you something.'

As Jonas opens the passenger door, Kestas looks around. The road is quiet. The nearest house is thirty metres away. The forest is thick on either side of the road. In the distance the very top of a block of flats peeps over the trees. Jonas passes him the bottle as he gets in. He takes another drink, half a mouthful. Jonas is ugly close up, black tooth in his smile and breath smelling of cigarettes and cabbage.

'Are you good at digging, Kestas?'

Kestas shrugs.

'You are big and strong. A husband. A father.' Jonas has his grin, the mocking smile on his face. 'My father told me today about a diamond necklace. It belongs to you and I.'

There is a silence. Jonas's mouth is curling into a cold smile. 'My father has worried about this for the last forty years. When the Nazis came to Ukena my father decided to help them. He hated the Jews, they were always taking everything. So father, the police chief of the town, meets the Germans when they arrive, says that the good people of Ukena will help them against the Russians and the Jews.'

Kestas sits listening, stomach churning. He knows that somehow his two uncles were involved in the killings, but not the details. His mother would never tell him.

'One week later, my father has a gun and a Labour National Guard uniform. The Jews in the town are very scared. The Nazis start to take the Jews to the forest. Bang! They shoot them all in the head. The Nazis are very happy with father's good work and say he can have any Jewish house in town. He takes the doctor's house, you know, the big one next to the bus station. Where the mayor lives now.

'So there is father, very happy with his new house. He cleans it out, gives the clothes and toys and books away, and gets mother to scrub it down and get the Jewish dirt out. But when he is going through all the junk he finds one photograph, and another, and another. All of them show the doctor's wife, Mrs Altmann, wearing a diamond necklace. Father looks for it everywhere. He pulls up the floorboards. Digs the garden. It drives him crazy.

'Then he remembers her in the forest. The Lithuanians were laughing because one German soldier was being sick. Mrs Altmann was screaming and screaming. They shot everyone before her, and the more she screamed the more they all laughed. She was the last Jew left. In the end, father shot her himself, tired of the screaming.

'So sitting in his new house, he thinks about when he killed her. They were the last Jews, and the Germans were in a rush to move on, so they didn't search them properly. Usually they would make them strip, check if they were hiding any jewellery. But on this occasion, there was no time. They had to shoot them as quickly as possible. The Germans had to move on to the next town on their list.

'So Father thinks about it, when he shot her. And the more he thinks about it, the more he is sure that she had the diamond necklace on her person. Father knows she is buried at the very top of the pit, so it wouldn't be too difficult to find it. He keeps waiting and waiting for the right moment. Then the Russians come back and he is sent to Siberia. For eight years, freezing his balls off, he thinks about this necklace. When he returns he has lost the house but he is more and more sure the necklace will be somewhere at the top of the pit. So he keeps waiting and waiting for the right moment. And thirty years later, sitting in a chair where he pisses himself twice a day, he tells me, the stupid old fuck.'

Jonas wipes his nose on the back of his hand and sighs in frustration. 'You are lucky your father is dead, Kestas. You are lucky you do not have to listen to such a stupid old bastard every day . . .'

Kestas is silent.

'I know where we have to dig. Chances are, we will find other stuff too. Jewellery, gold and silver. Stuff the Jews took to their graves with them. They have no need for it now. We have to be careful, but it shouldn't take long to find. The pits are not too deep. The deal is, you dig. It is our family legacy, but I found out about it. You get a percentage if we find it.'

Kestas glares at Jonas. 'No. Fuck you. I'm having nothing to do with it.'

Jonas looks over at Kestas, smile gone. 'Be sensible, Kestas.

Help me. Don't make a mistake.' Jonas smiles again. That smug, leering smile.

'What do you mean?'

'You are already in trouble. A subversive. Although now you do have short hair . . .'

Kestas watches Jonas, the way the humour has drained from his face, the coldness in his eyes.

'Kestas, you have a wife and a child. They love you and need you. They don't want you to disappear. You are something of a criminal already, according to my friends.'

Kestas stares at him, stares into his unrelenting eyes. Jonas is KGB. He can't believe it.

Jonas continues. 'Now, let's be reasonable about this. You dig, and my friends will leave you alone. I'll make sure you avoid re-education. I get the necklace, you go free. It's a good deal.'

Kestas is silent.

Jonas laughs. 'Good boy!' He turns the ignition key and the engine growls to life.

The car swings round and heads away from the town. The tremble of the motor runs through Kestas like a shiver of nerves. It is the warmest day of the year so far, but he feels cold. Jonas drums his fingers on the wheel as he drives. They turn off the main road, onto a gravel track. The lake appears, the same lake where Kestas's father drowned nearly twenty years ago. Jonas drives around the edge, car bumping and spitting up stones. Up ahead, the opening in the forest appears.

After a couple of minutes Kestas sees the turn-off towards the pit. It is a rutted, stony track. The wheels slide a little when they accelerate on the dry dust. Next to the entrance is a wooden effigy, carved in the image of a skeletal human wrapped in twisted barbed wire. The varnish has faded and it is pocked with woodworm holes. As they drive up the track the car shunts from side to side, spreading a cloud of dust in its wake. The windscreen is spotted with the grassy glue of dead insects, but this does not prevent Kestas from seeing the concrete archway ahead of them. Jonas takes his foot off the pedal and the car sidles to a halt. The silence hangs like a shroud on the forest. Jonas coughs, breaking the spell. The birds break into song when Kestas gets out the car.

Jonas opens the boot and hauls out a pick-axe, a rake and a spade. He begins to walk towards the archway. Kestas looks back down the track. 'What if someone comes?'

'When were you last here?'

'I was a child.'

'No one will come. No one ever comes. They either don't care or are too guilty.' Jonas grins.

Kestas follows him under the archway and into the clearing. At the side of the track a small animal scuttles in the undergrowth. Kestas glances over. A blackbird hops to and fro, looking for insects. The clearing is wide and overgrown with a thick tangle of grass. There is a natural path through the middle, splitting the graves into two rough halves. As he gets nearer he sees the long rectangular bald patches in the grass, raised bumps as though ten metre coffins are buried underneath. He stops at the first one and looks. The bald ground is a mixture of gritty sand and pebbles. A few weeds have taken root. In the middle of the clearing is a drooping yew tree. Underneath it is a stone plinth. He reads the inscription:

Jonas is shouting. Kestas looks over to the far corner where he is standing. 'Over here, Kestas! Come on. You were never interested in history at school,' Jonas laughs.

Kestas crosses the clearing, walking in a rut between two of the graves. The grass is mossy and springy underfoot. He feels as if he isn't here. Amazed by the thought that earlier this afternoon he was going home to Vaida and Erikas, going back to a normal life. And now this. But he knows he must do it, knows he must dig in this grave to save himself and his family.

The sunlight is fading. Jonas stamps his foot onto the grave, and twists his heel, breaking a layer of sandy soil. 'Right here,' he says. 'The earth is very loose. It won't take too long.'

Kestas shoves the spade in with the sole of his boot. He looks up for a moment. It is like the trees are watching him.

The darkness comes quickly as he digs. He moves back and forward, scattering soil onto the grass, a pendulum clocking the silent minutes. Jonas doesn't speak, just smokes cigarettes and occasionally lifts the bottle up from his feet to drink some vodka. Every so often his torchbeam slants across the pit, searching the overturned earth. Kestas ignores the bright light, just digs and digs, hoping that the mindless rhythm will hypnotise him, make him forget what he's doing. As he stops to wipe the sweat from his eyes, Jonas begins to yell excitedly.

'Look!' Jonas jumps over into the broken earth. He crouches and picks something up. He laughs and shines the torch into the palm of his hand. A gold tooth. 'They shot them in the head. Teeth everywhere! We're getting near.'

Kestas sticks the spade back in and twists. It hits something hard.

'Dig! Dig!' shouts Jonas.

Kestas thrusts his spade down and again he hits something hard. He feels with the spade and uses it as a lever. Something loosens, tearing itself from the ground. The torchbeam dances on his discovery. A ribcage, blackened with the wet, cloying soil. Kestas stares, frozen. The light moves away, leaving his eyes imprinted with an electric burn, fading into the blackness.

Jonas leans over the pit and begins to rake. A long, thick bone shakes itself loose, then another, then another. It is like the foundations are being ripped from the soil; grit slides in tiny avalanches into the imprints of the distorted skeletons. Jonas gets down on his knees and starts sifting the earth with his hands. His eager fingers locate another gold tooth; he holds the torch up close to it to check its gleam. In that moment Kestas sees the smile on Jonas's face, a smile that breaks impatiently. 'Help me, for God's sake!' Jonas shoves the rake towards him.

Kestas takes a step back away from the disturbed earth. He knows it is a step towards despair, but he turns away, mind made up, and starts to walk out of the clearing. The ground is soft under his feet, the breeze cool on his face.

'Kestas! Come back here you fucking idiot!'

He keeps walking; all around him he can make out the sketchy shapes of trees and bushes. The air smells damp and green, full of the quiet and unstoppable force of spring. He knows that the creatures of the forest will be watching him: all the mice and rabbits and half-sleeping birds will be eyeing him fearfully, waiting for him to pass and make the night theirs again. His head tilts back as he walks. Overhead the sky is a blanket of inky black, smothering the stars.

'Kestas! Get back here and help me you fucking prick!'

He feels sick, wants to bring up his lunch, spew out the fried sausage and eggs. Yesterday just now he was sitting in the kitchen with Vaida. Erikas was sitting on the floor playing with a rolled up ball of newspaper. The radio was on: it was The Beatles, 'Day Tripper'. They were all sitting around, happy. It was so normal and ordinary, but now the memory feels pristine, perfect, like a promise of an impossible happiness.

Jonas's torchbeam hits him square in the back, spilling his shadow in front of him like a nuclear flashprint burned into the forest floor. He keeps walking, shutting out the yells behind him and his shadow lengthens, until it stretches to nothingness and the light disappears.

*

The knock comes just before eight the following morning. Kestas lies on the bed staring at the ceiling, fully clothed. Vaida lies next to him, holding him. They have lain awake all night. Waiting. Waiting for the knock.

Kestas stands up. He puts on his jacket. Vaida gets up and pulls him close, crushing him tight against her. Their embrace is interrupted by another knock. Kestas gently removes Vaida's hands from his waist and leaves her standing with her hands over her face. He goes through to the hallway and opens the door, savouring these last moments in his home. On the landing are two policemen, and Jonas.

'Kestas Kovalenko? We are arresting you on suspicion of desecrating war graves.'

Kestas steps out, and as he pulls the door shut behind him, he sees Tomas watching him, standing in his pyjamas with his thumb in his mouth.

The morning air is cool. Fog wreathes the tower blocks and blurs the horizon, its vapour draping cobweb strands over the distant forest. He can feel the unseen faces peering from a hundred windows in the flats all around, the town holding its breath as another citizen is disappeared. As he gets into the back of the car, elbowed along the back seat by Jonas, he notices that he still has dirt under his fingernails, the broken soil of his homeland.

PAULO DA COSTA
Hell's Mouth Bay

We never carried ill intentions towards Camila Penca. We simply prayed for our village's old peace to be restored and, thank God, He answered our prayers.

Camila was born into a well-bred family in our respectable village nestled on the tusk-sharp escarpment of Hell's Mouth Bay. A village still standing with pride and resilience after centuries of Atlantic rage. Camila spent childhood in her own world. She climbed up and down the escarpment, collecting gull feathers, splashing in the tide pools, plucking at the sea urchins, *she loves me, she loves me not*, then, with the first tides of puberty, *he loves me, he loves me not*.

Some say that all along Camila displayed an inclination to stir up havoc. Surely there were instances of wickedness, as she had spied on people in their outhouses or stood on other girls' chests to help them muscle up breasts. But who has never been possessed by wicked moments?

Mostly, we blamed the late Ti Bernardino Mudo for leaving the mouth of his old well broad to the sky. Trapped at the bottom, the smells of the rotting wooden foundation, the sweet moss and the salty ocean mist tingling her nose, Camila crouched in a puddle, peering at a sky resembling a needle's eye. Not even the waves' consoling murmur found her ears. Gulls and rats were her only company. Gulls hopping from beam to beam above her head and sprinkling earth crumbs on her hair, rats scurrying over her body for a fish bone.

Lord, forgive us for such evil thoughts, but one would almost have wished Camila had never survived that cursed hole. We searched the land. We launched fishing nets and combed the bay, in the hope her body lay entangled in the sargasso. We peeked into the cleavages of rock for her trapped body. All without luck. Her mother waiting on the beach with the moon and the stars, wailed the child's body ashore, as months before she had waited for the breakers to return her husband. It was she who spotted the green balloon tied to the gull, swooping and diving above the cliffs, against the rising sun. Camila had carried a green balloon in her pocket since she was knee high, 'will lift me one day into the sky like Icarus,' she would sing.

The gull led us to Camila and we fished her out of the damp well. Everyone wanted to touch and kiss the girl. Mayor Ressaca, full of pomp and reeking of cologne, eeled through the pandemonium and covered her in kisses. His thunderous voice promised he would name a village lane after Camila, parallel to her father's, as soon as the new roads were paved in his next mandate. Padre Baptista blessed Camila, assuring her he had known all along through his prayers she was in the safe hands of God. Dona Branca told her she had prayed the rosary nightly and Camila would not have to worry about school work again. Camila fidgeted and sneezed. She told us to stop. She could smell our fishy lies. We laughed. A fall from such height was known to stir funny things in one's mind. Her wide terrified eyes focused above our heads and her steady sneezing went unnoticed in the midst of the tumult over her rescue.

After years of surrendering villagers to the sea and losing hope in miracles, we gathered for mass, thanking the Trinity and the Virgin Mary for protecting a Christian soul and returning a village child safely to our lap. Padre Baptista's homily reeled in the virtues of Christian faith. He assured the congregation that Camila's successful rescue was God's reward to the few spirits who attended his nightly rosaries and resisted the Devil's traps in Ti Inácio's tavern maids. The Devil tempted the flesh into dark holes. Camila began to sneeze relentlessly, crying 'Lie well.' The perplexed Padre Baptista on the pulpit blushed, and Sister Maria, in the choir, stared at her habit.

We stopped mass and wrapped Camila in a winter blanket assuming the dampness of the well had brought on her infernal sneezing.

Before re-assembling for mass we demanded that Camila confess her sins. We obliged her to purge any unattended sin that might have caused our Lord to inflict her with such penance. We huddled around the confessional. We heard her confide to Padre Baptista that she could smell a lie. Some lies hid, masked under expensive perfumes, others hid under cow manure. Dressed in perfume or cow manure, every lie carried the subtlest yet unmistakable stench of rotting fish, which triggered a gull-like cry from deep inside Camila's being. When she remembered the Act of Contrition we sighed, relieved.

Returning to the mass, we sniffed the air. There was no stench of rotting fish. Only the sweet beeswax candles dripping and the rose scent of incense from the altar. We could not even blame Rosária Cardo, the fishmonger. Rosária Cardo, who would rush into the pews late, wiping her hands on her hips, glistening sardine scales clinging to her skirt. But Rosária Cardo was away on her Friday run into neighbouring villages. At that moment likely balancing her wicker basket along a winding goat's trail.

Ti Raul said perhaps it was his fault. After changing into his Sunday clothes for mass, he had been unable to stop himself from checking the crab traps on his way to church. The smells might have clung to his best suit.

Padre Baptista exercised his God-given authority and led Camila by the wrist to the pulpit. Under the Virgin Mary's statue he tested Camila's claims. He began by telling her Adamastor, the sea-monster, was denned in our bay as was the commonly held belief. Camila's nose twitched upwards, faster and faster, until three sneezes bellowed out, accompanied with the cry 'Lie well,' announcing to us a lie had dropped in the village, wet as a splash of guano. Padre Baptista smiled approvingly. He also told her that one of the Virgin's three secrets at Fátima was the world's imminent end. Camila's sneezing rung through the church, echoing like three strikes of the church bell. Padre Baptista muttered his assent and blessed himself. He was convinced. At that moment we thought Camila was heaven's messenger, a blessing.

Padre Baptista finished mass with the choir ceaselessly singing in the background. He sacrificed his words of wisdom, but he knew it was best to fill the air with a storm of words.

That way he could always point his finger at the choir any time Camila's sneezing might threaten to ruffle the bible waters. Padre Baptista's inspired solution prompted our Hail Mary of thanks. Later, Mayor Ressaca, encouraged by Padre Baptista's success, never again discussed the village's budget without Dona Branca reading the newspaper aloud in the background.

As Camila slowly recovered from her ordeal in the well, she confided to us she could smell lies gathering above our heads the way we could see a summer storm gathering over the top of the Serra do Senhor Frutuoso.

Day or night, we had never a moment of peace. It was as if a thick fog had moved in from the sea and settled over the village. The trumpeting of Camila's nose echoed against the cliffs, down the cobblestone streets and entered a home without knocking. Even the whispers of husbands and wives in the matrimonial bed were not immune to Camila's nose. Ti Justa and Ti António, after fifty years happily married, cut relations as Ti Justa threw Ti António's pillow into the corral with the goats. In bed he had been whispering honeyed words, 'My sweet Justa, my life's true and only love,' just as a sneeze sounded, freezing their beads of amorous sweat. Ti António's mouth, caught in the open, left Ti Justa forever cursed with doubt. Husband or wife could never agree if the lie, like a crow of bad luck, perched in another bedroom or their own. Couples would argue into the black over who was lying and about what.

We started to walk around the village like ghosts, our eyes swollen, irritated at the least uphill difficulty. The Mudos and the Silvas, firmly entwined families from century-old blood alliances, refused to speak to one another and forbade their children from playing together. All because Marcelino Mudo, standing in line at the bakery, demanded aloud from Carolina Silva the yearly kiss she had promised him during their teenage dating years. Carolina Silva gathered her twin toddlers on each hip and stomped out yelling to Marcelino Mudo once and for good to keep his gossipy tongue to himself or go kiss the sea urchins instead.

We would not chance speaking alone. To avoid catching a tongue out of its element, conversations unrolled with everyone rallying at once. We didn't lend an ear to each other. The village affairs began to crumble. A tongue caught flapping during one of Camila's sneezing attacks was instantly sentenced to the fate of a sole on land – hung up to dry under a cloud of doubt. For Camila warned us, the seven deadly sins were like a deep well, and lying was the lid that prevented their expiation. Layers and layers of sins rotted in the dark of the deep and a sin was never born alone. There were always strings and bait.

Having a mere child flog us like sinners was not a fish-bone the village was prepared to swallow. That was between God and oneself. Sins were a private business and no one walked through life without netting a full catch. But when many people commit a sin, together, then we are talking evil and that is something else.

Ti Raul, mending the nets on the beach, suggested it wasn't poor Camila's fault. She was a celestial angel. A true guardian angel, keeping us on course, saving us from drowning in eternal hell. He insisted that if we only committed to tell the truth to each other we would find joy and peace. Marcelino Mudo, leaning on the prow of his boat, always ready to stir sand in the air with his stingray tongue, told Ti Raul his mussel-brain notions were crazy. Everyone needed cover from the punishing world. Ti Raul, pointing at the sea, held that we went fishing in the open, where there was nowhere to hide, facing wind, fog and rain, but we survived. Marcelino Mudo snorted he was forgetting the drowned. Ti Raul kissed the gold cross dangling from his chest and stared at the fog-shrouded sky before declaring it was also our ignorance that caused us to drown. No one had bothered to learn to swim. Ti António, until then silent, lifted his stocking bonnet to scratch his bald head and reminded Ti Raul that in fairness most of us didn't know we were not telling the truth because we had been whispering through nets for so long. The small fry lies, like the air we breathed, had always escaped harmlessly through the nets. Marcelino Mudo moored the conversation, suggesting we were being punished by God for old wrinkly sins.

We were nearing despair and might have committed something ungodly had we not set about bringing the peace of the village back to its due place among us. With Padre Baptista's blessing, candle light vigils gathered around Ti Bernardino's well and incessant prayers were said to cleanse the rotten spirits that infested the dark hole. We even winched Camila down on a rope while Padre Baptista blessed her and the well with the holy waters of the ocean, but to no avail. Her sneezing would not surrender. She bellied out in protest that it was the village and not she who needed to hang over the bottom of the rotten well to have a good look at themselves in the dark puddles. She insisted we were slippery eels hiding in the murky bottom. We lit more candles and prayed more fervently. Camila's last words were that we could never drown our conscience. The ocean waters returned things promptly. Poor child. We were trying to help.

The next morning the village woke up to silence. The fog had miraculously lifted. The ocean slept without a ripple, reflecting the blue of heaven. Even Esmeraldina, the young widow, who had sworn never to show her face to daylight opened her blinds a crack, curious about the oceanlike murmur of the crowd gathered in the square. Ti António remarked that the morning smelled of air after a storm, sweet and serene. Ti Raul, who had nearly drowned in his youth, said the still waters reminded him of the ocean's bottom. During sea storms, fishermen say the sea bottom remains calm, and that is the reason our drowned reach the shore with a peaceful smile, but with no eyes. The deep sea creatures steal their eyes. Eyes distract one from seeing the truth, seeing their way back to land. The sea creatures hide the eyes in tight-lipped shells where they harden into gleaming pearls only fit to admire one's vanity. Staring at the glimmering waters Marcelino Mudo said we had reached bottom on this affair with Camila. Everyone agreed.

Camila was nowhere to be seen. We searched without luck. Dropped fishing nets. Combed the bay from shoulder to shoulder. Night and day, Camila's mother kneeled on the beach wailing her spirit to heaven. She plucked at sea urchins, *hates me, hates me not.* Four of the strongest women in the village anchored her down as she wrestled, possessed by an urge to run into the ocean one moment, up the escarpment the next.

The gulls feeding out at sea shattered the crystalline mirror. An army of children with sling shots drove their cries away from Hell's Mouth Bay. One girl said she spotted a green balloon floating out to sea but we were all there and the morning light reflecting in the waters is known to play devilish tricks on the mind.

We will never know the mystery of God's wishes or the destiny of Camila Penca. We enjoy the old peace back in the village and have nailed down for good the mouth of Ti Bernardino's well.

LARI DON
Melon's 69p

The first time it was not premeditated.

She was squatting on the pavement retying her lace, not kneeling as the pavement was dirty and damp, but crouching with one foot flexed under her and the other balancing on its heel.

There it was, right in front of her. Inches away.

Melon's 69p

She just licked her finger and smudged it off.

Melon s 69p

She glanced furtively around her. No one in the shop doorway or on the pavement had noticed. She stood up faster than was good for her balance, tried to look inconspicuous, and strode off, forgetting momentarily her intention to buy green beans.

She was shocked at her own impertinence. Her finger had snaked out and removed the offending squiggle before her brain had even started down the familiar track of 'possessive or contraction, NOT plural'.

It hadn't been planned. It hadn't even been conscious. But now it felt liberating. She walked home without any vegetables for lunch but with a renewed sense of intellectual purpose.

There was one fewer offender in the blizzard of unnecessary apostrophes blighting the small shopfronts of Edinburgh. She had struck a blow for the English language. She had rescued one small sign from the sin of imperfect punctuation. She may have broken the law of the land (had she? she wondered) but she had upheld a higher law.

She was a punctuation pirate, a linguistic outlaw, a campaigner for clarity. A reiver of rogue apostrophes. A fruit shop fugitive. She stopped playing with this list when she realised she was mouthing softly to herself and attracting looks from passersby.

By the time she reached home, she was starting to doubt whether she had really achieved anything. When the price of melons changed, or it rained again, or when another more tasty bargain was on offer, or if a dog used the sign as a territorial marker, then the shopkeeper would commit another serious semiotic sin, and the melon would again own the 72p or the cabbage would possess the 40p.

Even more depressing, many of the shoppers wandering around Leith today would see her altered sign and feel superior to the poor ignorant foreigner who had gone and forgotten the essential apostrophe.

The next few times she passed along Great Junction Street, she looked furtively at the chalk board outside the fruit shop. The melons were no longer headline news. New potatoe's, vine tomato's and herb's all flaunted their apostrophes at her.

Could she brazenly stoop down again and remove the

offending mark? What had been so easily done once, without thought, was much harder when she had to plan it.

She considered undoing her shoelace before she left the house to have an excuse to kneel down, but was afraid she would forget she had done so and would trip over her own feet on the way down the road.

If she had a toddler with her, she could bend down beside it and use a spat-on hanky to clean its face, and just wipe off the apostrophe at the same time.

Even if she had a little dog, she supposed, she could stoop down to chat to it, or whatever dog owners do, and sneak a finger out to remove the chalk mark.

She was walking more stiffly and more slowly past the shop, conscious of the number of shoppers, shop assistants and delivery men surrounding her. All of whom could pounce if she attacked the sign.

Some days they were advertising more than one type of produce. So there was more than just one apostrophe. What kind of subterfuge would be needed to buy enough time to remove them all?

Why was this one sign annoying her so much?

After all, for years she had railed silently against the gathering hordes of misplaced apostrophes. Did people think that every word ending in '*s*' needed an apostrophe? Like a '*q*' needs a '*u*'? She had also been irritated at the profusion of capital letters appearing in the middle of sentences. Had the Germans won the war? She had tutted under her breath about quotation marks round random words in adverts and posters. To whom were they attributed, for goodness' sake? Her mutterings against these and other vagaries of the handwritten signs in small shops round Edinburgh had been no more than a benign mental wallpaper until her little incident last week.

She even walked along Great Junction Street one evening just before her bedtime, wondering if the shopkeeper left his sign out at night, and if there would be a chance under cover of darkness to correct the sign just the once more to put her mind at rest.

However, the street was almost as bright and busy as day, with pubs and fish and chip shops and off-licences. There was no privacy to make corrections, nor indeed had the shopkeeper left the sign out on the pavement. For fear of vandals or thieves, she supposed, then realised with a start that she had planned to vandalise it, to steal his apostrophe – it may be unnecessary to her, but to him it was a piece of chalk, a piece of time and indeed a necessary piece of the word 'melons'.

But without the press of people pushing her along, and the shopkeepers standing outside their doors, taking delivery of cardboard boxes or sorting their fruit, she felt a lot less inhibited about looking in windows, reading the signs on doorways.

What she saw both horrified her and gave her a warm sense of justification.

She had been worried that she was overreacting. But the evidence of crimes against coherence was everywhere.

One shop apparently thought it worth saying on an A4 sign: 'We also sell net curtain's.' The apostrophe no longer surprised her, but the utter banality of the marketing strategy amazed her. Until she thought that perhaps displaying net curtains would be rather hard – hung in the window, they would hide all the other goods. The ironing board covers and the nesting plastic boxes. So in order to attract the hordes of people wanting net curtains they would have to advertise in an unsubtle way.

She didn't sleep when she got home after her abortive night raid. She was examining her motives. Worried now that a single incident, a satisfying yet scary change from her routine, a moment of silent madness, was starting to dominate her life.

She had found she couldn't walk past that fruit shop without being drawn to the sign. She was glancing round at people to see if they were looking at her, judging to see if she had the seconds she would need to win another temporary victory against the misuse of language.

She had been finding herself drawn during the day to more and more streets filled with small grocers and scruffy charity shops, looking for bad grammar, spelling mistakes, unreadable layouts. She was torn between pleasurable wincing at a new twist of stupidity, an angry desire to rip the offending pieces of paper, plastic and board down and a cosy feeling of superiority over the ignorant.

Yet if it was ignorance she was trying to erase, rather than one tiny apostrophe, why didn't she beard the lion in its den? Explain to the perpetrator his minor yet significant crime. Offer him a free and friendly lesson in grammar and usage. The idea of an honest approach, rather than all this sneaking about at ungodly hours, appealed to her and with a glow of righteousness, she finally drifted off to sleep.

The next morning, she dressed carefully. Not too prim, like some deranged Victorian school mistress. Nor in khaki, like some urban terrorist. She tried very hard to dress casually, like an ordinary shopper who had just popped into a shop with a comment about apostrophes.

How did she normally dress to get her messages? Jeans and T-shirt? Leggings and jumper? Long cotton skirt and vest? When she thought about it, they all seemed contrived.

Eventually she decided to wear exactly what she had been wearing the previous week when she erased the apostrophe. Just as if she had nipped in that day, rather than taking ten days to come up with the idea and steel herself to carry it through.

So, a big baggy jacket, a pair of former office trousers, and ankle boots. No hat. Hats, however hard they try, can't be inconspicuous. They always make a statement.

She intended to have toast for breakfast, but misjudged the second shot in the toaster, the one to get it just right, and burned it slightly. She put it on her plate, considered buttering it anyway, but knew she would never eat it, so instead she picked it up, scrunched it like warm tissue paper in one fist and threw it on the lino. Staring at the black and brown crumbs, she thought, I'm in no state to explain the intricacies of the English language to an unwilling audience today.

Nevertheless, she picked up her keys and her wallet and marched out the door.

Her wallet was pretty light, prompting a tactical question. Should she buy something, and introduce the subject of grammar naturally into the conversation? But there never was conversation. Only an exchange of information:

'That's £1.12.'

'There you are.'

'Bag?'

'No thanks.'

'Thank you.'

'Thank you.'

So should she just walk in and say, 'Excuse me, but . . .'
And then what?

Should she wait until the shop was empty to avoid humili-
ating him (or herself?) or should she seek safety, and indeed
confirmation of her case, in a group of customers?

It suddenly seemed a long way to her local shop.

She practised simple explanations in her head: You only
need an apostrophe for two cases: the genitive or possessive,
like John's car (formerly 'John his car', or carriage perhaps,
but don't worry about that) or a missing letter or letters like
'it is' becoming 'it's' (but not when 'it' is in possession like
'its headlights', but don't worry about that). You don't need
apostrophes for plurals or for other words ending in 's'. Now as
the melons don't actually own the 69p, nor have you shortened
the word to fit it on the sign, you don't need an apostrophe. In
fact, as all you are likely to be doing is putting a noun and a
number on your wee board, you probably don't ever need apostrophes. Just don't use them. Just stop worrying about them.

Perhaps she should just stop worrying about them herself.
What was she doing? There are so many more important
things in the world, she told herself. But clear communication
was the basis of human relationships and ambiguity was its
enemy. Apostrophes are there to clarify. We have so many
ways of using 's', and so many ways of shortening common
words. The apostrophe is there to prevent misunderstanding.
Like an antibiotic, she muttered, it loses its power if it is used
too often.

Anyway, it was annoying her, and making her lose sleep, and all she wanted to do was tell the bloke in a friendly way that he was abusing the English language and breaking rules made by better men than him. And there would be an end to it.

She stopped short at the fruit shop. The sign read:

Special offer Today

Garlic 49p a lb

She started walking.

Deflated. Relieved. Cheated.

She wandered around Leith Walk, Easter Road and Duke Street for a while. Looking intently at shop windows, pavement A-boards, stencilled Ford vans. She counted, under her breath, thirty-four unnecessary apostrophes, twenty-seven misplaced capital letters and half a dozen words or phrases in quotation marks for no good reason.

One of the few shops with no grammatical errors in its advertising was a small office supplies shop. She entered, and spent her few remaining pounds on some Tipp-Ex, a black felt tip, a small pot of red paint and a wee brush.

Scarcely admitting to herself what she intended to do, she stepped back out onto the street.

And there across the road was the best example yet:

Charle's and Son

Baking since 1936

She laughed out loud, with joy and wonder.

It was a professional shopfront. Bright yellow background and an elegant dark green script. The shop had paid someone to make this, and to fix it above their door and window. Why had no one noticed? Why had no one said?

It was a gift. A sign from whatever lay above or below.

She looked round for a ladder, expecting there to be one to hand just because she needed it and the situation was so right. But there was no skiving window cleaner or anachronistic chimney sweep in the area.

She would have to improvise.

Like any stretch of shopfronts in the rundown bits of Leith, there were several house clearance, fifth-hand furniture shops nearby, with their wares littered on the pavement.

She crossed the road diagonally, heading for the clearance shop two doors down from the bakery, where she picked up a middling sized gateleg table and a spindly dining chair. She turned and without looking back, carried them awkwardly but quickly to the baker's. She opened up the gateleg, placed the chair firmly in the centre and clambered up using the shop's window ledge.

It was a low shopfront, added onto the older building behind, so she could now reach the sign by stretching. From her pocket she got the brush and the paint. After a dicey moment using the pointed brush handle to prise open the paint lid, she did not hesitate.

A bold stroke of red through the whole word 'Charle's', then rewriting it in smaller but clear letters underneath: 'Charles'.

She hadn't heard a thing while engaged in the exercise. No buses or children or mobile phones. But now that she had corrected the sign, the full sounds of city life crashed in again, overlaid with some new shouting.

She turned to get down. Balancing carefully, she descended, but only achieved the stability of the window ledge and the pavement at the cost of knocking the chair to the ground.

She turned to the loud woman in the apron.

'You didn't need the apostrophe.'

They were both silent for a moment.

She righted the chair and set off down the road, smiling briefly at the man in the door of the furniture shop.

Past the next bus stop, she paused outside a newsagent and used Tipp-Ex to alter an A4 sign reading 'We sell all Types of phone card's'. She walked on.

GARETH GOODALL
Salvage

This is not a cry for help.

1

Pornography was making me sick. Not psychologically sick, though I fear that I already fall into that category, but physically sick. Ill. Unwell. Poorly, although that word makes me sound about thirty years younger than I am. I normally stayed for longer, for the harder films, but I was already starting to feel truly nauseous as I wiped the cum from my hands and prepared to sidle out of the sweaty cinema in my usual ashamed shuffle. The vile, metallic tang was there, firmly lodged in the pit of my stomach, twisting in my veins and coursing through my body. Urging me to vomit some of my guilt onto the accomplice streets. Into the gutter. As I stood up from my seat the projection of the girl's screaming face was splayed across my eyes, my face, like an intricate and elaborate tribal tattoo. On screen, hugging my shadow, a barely sixteen-year-old girl was being roughly introduced to a third man and I was thinking about my wife, my son, my job. My father, with his sternly disapproving chin and judgmental furrowed brow.

I was wondering what they would think of me, stood there in the dark, during the middle of the morning, hoping my sperm had not squirted onto my trousers. Self-loathing is an emotion that by its very definition should be confined to the self, but right then, as heaving flesh flicked across my eyes, I loathed every dark silhouette that I glimpsed hunched over in their chairs, stifling groans. *I* was one of *them*. Sad, ashamed and washed up, with a shrivelled cock and sticky hands. The dirty mac brigade. A sinister figure of fun and shame and disgust. I wondered if they too were beginning to consider whether they would be recognised as they left the cinema. By a colleague or a neighbour or their wives. At least I was safe from my wife. I just had to lie to her. And to watch as her eyes darkened and dimmed by the day.

I was in this frame of mind when I saw the business card. Absently placed on the plastic easy-to-wipe seat like a whore's calling card, I picked it up curious to see which unfortunate wanker had dropped it. I wanted to put a name to the shadowy figures around me, to gain some comfort from their identity so I would not feel so alone in my shame. In the darkness I could not quite read it and as I tried to hold it closer to my eyes there came a hoarse shout from the back:

'Hey! Sit down!'

I slipped the card into my suit pocket and left hastily.

My usual routine was to put my head firmly within my collar and to walk quickly down the nearest sidestreet I could find. Having performed this procedure I stopped on a quiet cobbled road, to lean against a decrepit wall. I looked behind me but nobody that mattered had seen me. Nobody was following. Outside the darkened cinema the world was carrying on as normal. Everyday business. I reached into my suit pocket for the card. I was interested as to who would be so careless. Your identity, your details, were things to be very careful with when you visited the sort of places I did. I found myself mildly disappointed, however, to find that the card did not belong to a business man. Instead, firmly embossed on the ivory weave was a logo:

S.	A.	L.	V.	A.	G.	E.
l	n	u	a	v	l	n
o	g	s	n	a	u	v
t	e	t	i	r	t	y
h	r		t	i	t	
			y	c	o	
				e	n	
					y	

Helping you to help you.

I read the flipside to the card with gathering interest and called them later that night. Two days later, I am sitting in their office at the very top of the Canary Wharf tower, on a day when I should have been working and occasionally masturbating about my secretary in the toilets.

2

On the wall above the reception desk the same logo is formed in black, 3D-effect letters, like a mission statement. The reception area is a vast minimalist design, a polar landscape. In fact, apart from the reception desk there is only the large black leather sofa I am sitting on and a glass coffee table, placed just far enough away so that I cannot reach it with my feet. The room feels bare, sanitised, and the air-conditioning has removed any trace of smell or scent. From where I am sitting I can see out of the windows that make up one whole side of the tower. The views are amazing and I study it like a child to try and hide my nerves. A young black woman, friendly but not too much, sits behind the reception desk in a red suit, apparently doing very little. She tells me to wait for a 'Mister Garblie'.

I sit cracking my fingers and tapping my brown boater shoes against the white tiled floor. On the coffee table there is a stubbed out cigarette lying next to an unsightly ash smudge, blurred against the glass. Somebody who had to have a cigarette despite the obvious lack of an ashtray, I think, understanding. Smoking has never been my thing, in fact I loathe it, but it felt good to see a trace, a remnant, of a previous visitor, however anonymous they may be. I stare at the floor and wonder if I should have come.

I guess you could call it an addiction, pornography. But I did not just stop at that. Cinemas, videos, live-girl shows, one-on-one dances, peephole booths, sex toys, magazines. The lot. Then I moved on from the drab, pre-recorded sex lines and started to call real girls. Girls that I could talk dirty to. From there it was not long before I was calling girls that I could invite to shamefully seedy and anonymous hotel rooms.

I'd ask to watch them, to touch them, to slap them, to fuck them. Anything that I could think of. Nothing was too low or embarrassing. Eventually it became more frequent and I found myself classifying places according to whether its telephone boxes carried the advertisements of the local whores. Holborn, Embankment and Oxford Street: yes. Faringdon, Bank and Canary Wharf: no. And then, when this became the norm, I would ask them for more. I've been tied up, slapped, bullied, shouted at, tortured, fucked. I repeatedly demeaned myself. It seemed to satisfy something. A longing, buried deep within, but itching, itching. When it was over I would sometimes sob until my throat bled but eventually the longing would return and I would be back, signing into another hotel under one of my false names. So that was why I was there. I was desperate.

The sound of leather soles clipping the tiles disturbs my thoughts and I look up to see a smartly dressed, sun-tanned man with a huge smile walking over towards me. The distance from the door he comes from to where I am sitting is so large that I become uncomfortable and avert my gaze to study my shoes. When he reaches me I am feeling sick with nerves but I stand and he extends a brown, manicured hand.

'Hi there, hi there,' he says warmly, shaking my hand as I rise from the chair. 'Darius Garblie. Nice to meet you.'

'Yes, hello,' I say anxiously.

'Come with me,' he says and walks off towards a set of double doors to the right of the lobby.

'Did you get here okay?' he asks.

'Erm, yes' I stammer, nervously. I am back to being fourteen, mumbling and awkward, yet the way he is acting, this could be a business meeting over in the City and I could be presenting my four-year plan for development.

'Some people have trouble on the Jubilee line,' he says, pushing through another door and heading down the white corridor on the other side, 'you're lucky'.

'I, errr, caught the light railway,' I say, trying to look through the slivers of window of some of the doors we pass. I catch glimpses of white shirted young men, staring moronically into computer screens. Garblie hurries me on, down the tunnel-like corridor and through various fire doors. We briefly pass a pair of smartly dressed young men standing beside an elevator door. As we pass I hear one of them ask the other if he is 'going up'.

'Is there another floor above this one?' I ask Garblie, curiously, as we pass through another fire door.

'No,' replies Garblie, innocently. 'This is the top floor. The view is fantastic, isn't it?'

We go through a blank door into a small, white room containing a desk and two chairs, placed facing each other across the desk. Next to one chair place there is a notebook and a clipboard and Garblie moves to this place and motions for me to 'take a seat'. I do, but I'm feeling awkward, my body tense.

'You can relax, Mr James,' Garblie says, affably, as he pulls the pad of paper towards him. I notice that there are scribbles written on the notepad already. 'I understand that you're nervous. Everyone is. It's natural.'

He pauses and gives me an understanding smile, before adding: 'Maybe it would help if I told you something about the process. I believe you have already spoken to a member of our new business team?'

I nod, and am about to confirm when I realise that I have forgotten the person's name, which is odd, as I have a good memory.

'I'll quickly take you through it then,' he says.

As he talks I am able to look at him for the first time. He has a long, sloping face with small beady brown eyes and a wave of dark, blow-dried hair swept along the top of his angular head. A pair of silver glasses sit delicately on his arching nose and his smart, navy suit is immaculately finished with a stark white shirt and a bright red tie. What I notice most, however, are his hands, which he manipulates constantly to emphasise a point. Brown nimble fingers hang off long, slender hands and every point, every full stop, seems to somehow be manifested into those digits so that they dance a vigorous vocabulary waltz through the air. He would make a good puppeteer.

'We are a Company that specialises in helping people manage their lives, Mister James. We analyse any problems there may be, in a frank and honest way, and then offer a solution to suit that person's needs. We operate on a similar basis to a Management Consultant, to put it in terms you may be familiar with. We aim to provide and implement a solution that enables a client to benefit most from a particular situation. Obviously this was explained to you over the phone.'

I nod but feel reassured to hear it again. The phone call

had been so difficult to make but I had instantly felt better. Relieved. Almost free.

Garblie continues. 'We will start with a general talk about your problem – and I use the word problem with some hesitation, Mister James, because we are all human – and then we will go on to discuss our solution. What I must stress, Mister James, is that I am not here to censor or judge. We will leave that to others. You have your free will and must use it. I should also add, of course, that everything you say will be kept in confidence. My only interest is in helping you to help you.'

He stares at me and raises one eyebrow, in part to see if I have any questions but also because he knows that I am sold, that I have already spent half an hour on the phone with a colleague and that I am desperate. He can surely see that, at least.

3

S.A.L.V.A.G.E. was, according to the voice on the phone, set up for precisely my kind of condition. 'An alternative to the Priory' was the way they had described it, half-joking. The Company aimed to help people who were struggling, to whatever degree, with 'certain aspects of their lifestyles'. Most of these aspects could be traced back to the seven deadly sins, an archaic term, they assured me, but one which was still relevant today. According to them, the sole objective of the Company was to attempt to salvage something from the problematic and possibly destructive lifestyle that was currently being led. Once I had given them the basic details they had been very understanding and had said that S.A.L.V.A.G.E. had dealt with many similar cases with a near 100% success rate. The next day a Company information pack arrived in a non-identifiable brown envelope and I called that night to make an appointment.

In the room, Garblie is writing as we speak, making notes. He had checked that this was okay, and I had allowed it once I had been assured that it was standard practice. It had been very difficult to begin talking to Garblie but once I started it became difficult to stop. It is not an easy task to keep things hoarded to yourself, as though your problems were fine wines and I was one of those people who could not resist drinking their collection. It was nice to give some of it away. The hardest part had been to tell him about the extents to which my problems had gone. I expected him to be surprised by some of the things I mentioned but he greeted every announcement with an understanding nod and a sympathetic smile, waiting for me to finish before asking questions.

When I finally finish Garblie taps his pen on the desk, like a cigarette.

'And what sort of effect is it having on your social life? On home?'

I pause and grind my teeth. 'That's the main reason I am here, really,' I say.

'I see.' He doesn't add anything more. Just waits, lets the silence hang.

'My wife is,' I start but then don't know how to end it. 'Not very well,' I conclude.

Garblie nods. 'Dying?'

'Yes.'

'Cancer?'

I nod, cautiously. 'How did you . . . ?'

Garblie shrugs innocently. 'Just a guess, Mister James. Just a guess.'

'Of course. Sorry.'

Garblie shrugs again, affably.

I look at my hands for what feels like a long time. 'My wife has six months left to live. She can't even speak properly anymore. I hate having to lie to her. I can't do it anymore. I don't want to have to spend the rest of her life lying to her like some sort of . . .'

'Cheat,' finishes Garblie.

'Yes. A cheat.'

Garblie nods and the room fills with an unbearable silence as the guilt hangs there, a raised guillotine.

'How do you think she would feel about your lifestyle?'

Despite myself my eyes are getting watery. 'I think she would worry about my ability to bring up our son after she has gone. She would worry about my capabilities as a father. She would be angry, of course, and upset but I think her first concern would be for my son.'

Garblie nods. 'She would be justified, Mister James.'

I nod and then realise that it isn't a question.

Garblie starts again but I interrupt him. 'Do you think you could call me something else,' I ask, 'rather than "Mister James"? "Gareth" or something.'

Garblie smiles. 'Of course. I apologise.'

There is a pregnant pause during which time I feel Garblie looking at me inquisitively.

'Is there any reason for that request? Or do you merely find it impersonal? Most people seem to prefer it that way.'

'It's nothing to do with it being impersonal,' I say, and then feel like I should add something. 'I always think of my father as "Mister James". He would never find himself in this position,' I state, finally.

There's another long pause. 'Why do you think that is?'

I crack my fingers noisily, feeling agitated.

'Is this about me or my family, Mister Garblie?'

'It's about you' he says simply and then waits.

I sigh and look at the ceiling. 'My father was a Judge. A very senior one and a very serious one too.'

'How do you mean?'

I'm vaguely aware that Garblie is making notes but I ignore it. 'He was very strict in his ideas about decency and discipline,' I say. 'You know, no girlfriends allowed upstairs, that sort of thing. My mother said it was because of his job. We couldn't have any scandal attached to our family, she said.'

'Did you get on with him?'

I stop to think, to choose my phrase. 'He was a good man, in many ways,' I say, 'but we were never very close. He was always very distant and stern. Again, my mother blamed his job. But he was also very strict. Very strict. When I was twelve he found some pornographic books under my bed. My friend from school had given them to me. Nothing outrageous. Not like now. But that didn't matter. Not to him. He beat me so hard, so badly, that he cut my face – I've still got the scars – and then we went outside and burned the books in the garden. Covered them in lighter fluid and set them alight.'

Garblie seems to understand. He has stopped writing and is looking at me sympathetically.

'This is weird,' I say, and now my eyes are starting to water and I'm wrestling with my chin, 'because I've never told anyone that before.'

Garblie nods. 'Your father's dead now?'

I nod and wipe at my eyes.

'Don't be upset, Mister James, please. This is the hardest thing you will ever do, but it is necessary, Gareth. It is necessary,' Garblie says, and for one minute I think he might reach over and hold my hand, but he doesn't.

'What about *your* job, Gareth? You're a Managing Director. A large publicly funded Company. Position of responsibility. Does your problem have any effect on it? Miss many days at work? Any inappropriate behaviour?' Garblie raises an eyebrow quizzically, his pen poised.

'Yes. I miss quite a few days at work.'

'And the inappropriate behaviour?'

'I didn't say there was any.'

'But there is, isn't there?'

I look at my hands. 'Yes.'

Garblie lets me suffer and holds the silence. I feel compelled to break it.

'I masturbate about my secretary in the toilets.' I have said so much, admitted so much, I may as well lay it all out.

'Did you employ your secretary personally?'

'Yes.'

'Because she can type at sixty words a minute? Or because she has nice tits and a firm ass?'

'Yes,' I stutter.

'Which one?' he asks, pleasantly.

'She can't type at all,' I murmur and then stare at the wall to the right of Garblie, lose myself in its glazed sheen.

The questions continue for another half an hour. I recall various experiences, some of which I had not thought about for years. Pained abstentions, sobbing regressions. Eventually Garblie puts the pen down next to the pad, rests his elbows on the table and smiles amiably.

'Well done, Gareth. That was hard, I know, but the worst is over. We can help you now.'

I sniff and wipe at my nose and he watches me before leaning backwards casually.

'Let me ask you a question, Mister James. How many times in your past have you thought: "Never again. That's it. I'm not going to put myself through this again"?'

'A few times. Quite a lot.'

He nods. 'You see, this is the problem. Any sin can be cured, can be stopped. You have already demonstrated a desire to do this. The difficulty is keeping it that way. It will always be an area of weakness. A fault to be fallen back on. What we will try and do is make sure that this does not happen. Do you know what the term "to repent" actually means?' I shake my head. 'I'm not religious.'

'You don't have to be,' he adds, seriously. 'It means "to turn around". What if I could offer you a way of curing yourself, of turning yourself around and never having to fall back on your weakness? What if I could offer you the chance of your life back? Forever?'

I'm frowning, unsure. 'I don't understand how this would

be possible. I'm sorry, I'm just not sure how it could work? You're not going to recommend surgery are you?'

Garblie laughs good-naturedly. 'No, no, no Mister James. We're not living in the 1950s now. As I said before, you must have your free will or else it means nothing. No, what I want to offer you is a personally tailored solution for your needs. Every client we have receives a different treatment, depending upon their problem and their situation. I believe that we can help you, Mister James. It just depends upon whether you want it.'

I stare at my hands. The bleak white light of the room is giving me a headache.

'I want it.' I say, which is, of course, the correct answer.

4

I'm led out of the room by Garblie, who strides in front of me carrying his clipboard like a doctor, his pen stuck into the front pocket of his suit. We go down the corridor and through a white door on the left. The room is about the same size as the one that we were just in except there is no table or chairs and a strange, antiseptic smell is lingering in the air, like in a hospital. A further white door leads out of the room from the opposite wall. I turn to Garblie as I hear him lock the door we just came through. He sees my alarm and smiles warmly.

'Nearly there now,' he exclaims, failing to explain the locked door.

I gulp and say nothing.

He takes me by the arm and leads me over to the door. I

look at Garblie, who is smiling, and then turn to the door. At the top is the logo:

S	A	L	V	A	G	E
l	n	u	a	v	l	n
o	g	s	n	a	u	v
t	e	t	i	r	t	y
h	r		t	i	t	
			y	c	o	
				e	n	
					y	

Following that are written two sentences:

'Flee from sexual immorality. All other sins a man commits are outside his body, but he who sins sexually sins against his own.'

'But he that shall endure unto the end, the same shall be saved.'

Garblie puts his arm across my chest, like a barrier. 'Through that door you will find the cure to your lust, Gareth. Through that door. I need to just make sure that you are absolutely definite that you want to go through with this.'

I stare at the door and he mistakes this for indecision.

'Think about what you get up to in those sleaze pits. The filth, the shame you feel afterwards. Then consider the idea of salvaging something from that life.'

I feel sick with nerves. I feel a nervousness that borders on excitement. 'I need help,' I say.

Garblie removes his arm and I push the door.

5

Garblie comes over after my legs have buckled and I have finished retching and dry vomiting so hard that my eyeballs felt like they were about to burst or bleed. He squats down in front of me and smiles. He has locked the door and now there is just the two of us, locked in a collage of black and white and colour photographs that are pasted all over the walls. They vary in quality and focus but it is fairly easy to make me out in the vast majority of them. In cinemas, in peep shows, at brothels, in the work fucking toilet, cock in hand. Just about everywhere I've ever been. Even the bondage is in there. I can see myself getting fucked. They've also paused the videos on the widescreen televisions and now I'm locked, frozen, in an animalistic sexual position with a variety of anonymous women. If this were not enough, the tape, which had been previously playing me the sounds of aggressive sex, is now on a loop so that I can hear myself repeatedly asking: 'Can I fuck you?' I am vaguely aware of a long despairing moan, like a wounded animal, and I realise it is me and I'm weeping. Howling.

When I recover, Garblie is still there, squatting like a vulture. He cocks his head and looks into my red eyes and I stare back at him wearily. I don't know what to say but Garblie waits patiently.

'I don't understand,' I say, finally.

'You're cured, Mister James. This is our solution.' He smiles and spreads his palms.

'But I don't understand how . . . ?' I motion towards the pictures and the room.

Garblie waves away the question. 'That doesn't matter. No, what matters is that you can now walk free from your addiction. You'll never go back.'

'How can you be so sure?' I spit.

Garblie laughs. 'Come on, Mister James, you wouldn't want this material to become available to the public, would you? To the press? This is what you wanted. Permanence.'

'I don't believe you would do it.'

'Well, that's up to you, Mister James,' Garblie says, excitedly. 'Again, this is nothing if it is not about free will.'

'Fuck you, Garblie! You can't do this!'

He's smiling now. A matador standing over the enraged but dying bull. There's no fight left. 'Think what you like, think what you like. Let me ask you though, Mister James, how sure you can be that those MPs and celebrities that are suddenly uncovered as paedophiles or bondage queens or homosexuals have not paid these very offices a visit?'

I look at the floor and pull at my hair, a dull realisation forming. 'I can't understand how you got all of this!'

'I understand your frustration,' he says, placidly. 'It isn't our business to explain these things to you, Mister James. It should be fairly obvious.'

I stare at him, dumbfounded and dull-eyed.

Garblie sighs and leans forward. 'Who, exactly, do you think places those ads in telephone boxes? Which organisations do you think manage massage parlours and cinemas and shows? Do you think they would be tolerated if they did not serve some dual function?'

'Why me, though? Why?' I shout.

'Because you needed us, Gareth. Remember, you called us. The majority of our business comes from people seeking us, not the other way round.'

I shake my head, dumbstruck, wondering if this can be happening. Flattening myself against the floor, sobbing, gasping, a mess, and all of this time a thousand groaning faces stare down at me.

6

In reception Garblie leads me to the desk and smiles at the receptionist, who looks back at us, smiling inanely. I'm wondering how much she knows.

'Could you get Mister James's coat, Laura?' asks Garblie, politely.

'I didn't have one.'

Laura smiles and wishes me 'Goodbye'.

I nod at her and then turn to Garblie. He extends his hand. I don't shake it.

'Well done, Gareth. It was a pleasure working together. If you should ever need further help, do not hesitate to call me.' He hands me a business card that I don't take. Eventually Garblie returns it to his suit pocket and smiles. 'Well, maybe we'll be in touch with you.'

I stare him in the eyes and then turn, feeling unsteady, wondering if I can make it all the way to the door that leads to the elevators. When I get there I hear him shout me, and when I turn he is virtually upon me, as though he had been following closely behind.

'One more thing, Mister James!' He hands me a brown A4 envelope.

'You don't need to show me anything more,' I say, not taking it.

Garblie just stands there, holding his arm outstretched. Gingerly I take the envelope.

'Open it,' he urges.

I swallow hard and then cautiously peel away the loosely stuck down flap and slide the contents out on to my hand. I grimace, expecting to see more pictures of myself but that is not what I see. The photograph is not quite right, the room settings too austere, the women too classy, the picture too grainy. My father looks young in the photos, or at least, younger than I remember him. His proud, legal chin is jutting out, straining as he fucks and his eyes are locked tight in a grimace as he grips one of the anonymous women. His comb-over is hanging down the side of his face almost comically, but he's oblivious. To everything.

'Your father came to us shortly before you were born,' says Garblie, as I slide the photographs back into the envelope. 'He was concerned about his behaviour. As I recall, he was worried that you would be a girl.'

I reseal the envelope and hold it firmly, giving Garblie one last look before turning and heading for the door.

'I just wouldn't be too hard on him for the way he was!' Garblie shouts after me.

I don't say anything but push my way through the door and leave in a trance, as though I'm not really there and everything around me is not real, like a digitally altered photograph.

7

On the light railway, heading home, I turn to watch the spire of Canary Wharf fade from view as the train ducks low beneath the platform tracks into the corrugated iron fences of All Saints' scrap yards and brick merchants. As it disappears out of sight the last I see of it is the pyramid roof, pointing upwards towards the sky, its aviation light flashing on and off, on and off.

A sign on the train catches my attention and I feel like reading it to all the names-on-a-list that sit around me. *For your own safety, CCTV is in operation.* It almost makes me want to cry with laughter.

I go home, to lie to my wife and to watch as her eyes darken day by day.

ELAINE HOLOBOFF
Second Coming

'"Forgive me Father, for I have sinned," that is what he said. Can you imagine? To me.' The man sat down laughing, his black robe making the sound of a sheet snapping in the wind as he pulled it in front of his body. Shoes clapping the stone floor.

'It is irrelevant, what he said. What is he doing at confession anyway?' The chair slides close to the oak table and a leather bound book slams onto the wood, scattering a pile of papers. 'We have decisions to make. Where are the others?'

'Here they are. Brothers, welcome. Five chairs here, five there.' Father Roy swings his arms wide above a small computer, indicating each side of the table. 'Coffee and whisky are coming shortly. We are sorry about the hour, but it seems that . . . it seems the time has come for us to move on the urgent matters of our last discussion. A final result must be determined tonight. The Council is waiting for our judgment. They want the files closed. Tomorrow.'

Black sheets snap again, and again as the brothers take their seats, chairs scraping. Throats clearing.

'Why, may I ask, is the Council pressuring us after eighteen years? The last time we met, in Rome, two years ago, was it not, they said it was a matter we needed to begin, and I must stress, *begin*, to have some thoughts on. At that time there was not even any discussion of identities, nor the age and character of the subjects. The Council seemed ignorant of, or perhaps uninterested in, the most basic details of the project. And now they want a decision. Tonight no less. It is clearly impossible given the circumstances. Impossible.' Brother Antonio sits down, slides Father Roy's computer over two inches to make room for his notepad, then jumps up again to open the shutters on the window. The salt wind of the Scottish coast comes in through the opening, thick and wet.

Bishop Constantine, eyes focusing on his pile of papers and books, places his hands slowly, palms down, in front of him. 'Brother Antonio, this is not a decision that has been rushed upon us. You are in full knowledge of the facts. You are aware that questions have been raised. Not only in Rome, but in the local community. Questions about the deaths of the ten. Ten in as many years, the most recent only last year. It is too much. Of course it has nothing to do with us. We bear no guilt. Nonetheless suspicions have developed about the Order itself. This cannot continue. A decision will be made tonight and conveyed to the Council in the morning. If we cannot reach a consensus, we will vote.'

'How is it that this decision is left to us?' A voice from the table middle.

A rare flower, Bishop Constantine's patience. He plucks at it. Sits upright in his chair. Speaks slowly. 'There is no longer anyone left in Rome who knows the full details of the project. The Council knows little, except that the files must be closed. Archbishop Giovanni headed the Curia's extraordinary

Science Council in the year 2005, and it was under him that a special, shall we say . . . secret, branch of the Council was established in order to look into the problem of the relics. As you know the Archbishop died thirteen years ago, only five years into the project. The special branch could no longer explain its existence. Sometime later it was disbanded for "irregularities". Files were destroyed. Since then, of this most of you are *not* aware, we have been functioning more or less autonomously. There have been no instructions. Until now.'

'Why not leave well enough alone? There are only the three left. We can carry on as we have.' A voice on the far right side.

A hand smooths back the grey hair on Bishop Constantine's head. His body leans forward. 'There is a certain Cardinal. He has been in a position to maintain an interest in the project. He has knowledge. Of the rationale for the project. Of the developments. Of the deaths, and their scientific explanations. It is he who demands a final decision on the matter. He has conveyed this to the Council, and the Council has contacted us. You will understand his position. The project has been a failure, and any evidence would be . . . would be controversial. As we discussed previously, there appear to be only three options. Brother Malcolm, review these for us please.'

'My duty is my pleasure Bishop Constantine. Simply put, the three considerations are as follows. One, to continue with the present situation. We discussed bringing the subjects into the Order and letting them live out their days among us and those who follow us. To make them as indistinguishable as possible. To know them as they know themselves. Members of this community. Two, send the subjects away to as yet undetermined locations. Here we decline further responsibility for their lives and fates. This would require that each subject be relocated in different places to forestall any interaction between them. Three, death, if we judge this to be justifiable within the guidelines of the Church. In this case we must determine time, place and method.'

'Brothers, Father Roy, it is with the greatest regret that I must tell you . . . option one is no longer possible.' Bishop Constantine pulls a file from under the leather book and feels the weight of the cream coloured paper as he lifts it out. It rasps against his smooth skin. 'The Cardinal has issued further demands. This morning. The Order is to be disbanded. Brothers, you are to travel to Rome for instruction within the fortnight, and report specifically to the Cardinal. He will ensure your safety and your future. He is grateful for your loyal participation in the project.'

Outside the wind from the coast picks up. The shutters slam against the outside wall. Slam again. Again. Brother Antonio pushes his chair back, a sigh against the stone, and he goes to the window to shut out the night air.

Some minutes later, a voice from the middle, left side of the table. 'The Order has been in existence for over five centuries. Life in this wilderness has been difficult. However we undertook this burden with joy. And now we are to move on? To where? With whom?'

'Another wilderness awaits. You must accept this with joy as well. You will be taken care of.' Bishop Constantine slides the paper back into the file.

The door opens and the smell of coffee comes into the room. Two brothers wordlessly place trays on the table and leave, closing the door behind them. Whisky, coffee, sugar, milk, oatcakes, white cheese, shelled walnuts, fruit. The glare of yellow pears on the tray assaults the eyes of the men. Misplaced succulence. A wrong order. Not for the evening at hand. Perhaps for a ringing morning when the birds call in the pines. No one touches the bright fruit.

'May I?' Brother Edgar pours out small thimbles of whisky and places them alongside cups of coffee which are distributed down the table to each man. Small plates of oatcakes and cheese are taken by some as the tray is pushed along.

Father Roy reaches for a plate and fills it with cheese slices and five walnut pieces. After sipping his coffee he picks up his fork and tastes the salt of the cheese. He follows this with several walnuts, fingered absently, then thrust into his mouth. His mouth turns bitter. 'Ahhhh.' He spits the walnuts onto his plate and grabs the bowl of brown pieces. 'These are foul! Foul! Take them out of here!'

Father Roy's eyes rest on a flat winged moth, long and pin-headed, flying upwards from the mound, its wings spreading out like a tiny fan. It is followed by another and then another. The insects are surprised by the disruption. Father Roy's fingers flick the nuts over, uncovering white cotton threads joining piece to piece. Black flecks are embedded in the convoluted surface of the walnuts. The moths flutter around. Placeless. Roy smashes his hand on a moth that rests on the table. His fingers come away. They are dusted with the powder of the moth's wings. He wipes his hand on his garment where a white streak is left, picks up his plate, and dumps the contents on top of the bowl of walnuts, cheese draping the worm filled food. The bowl is quickly taken away.

Moments pass as coffee and whisky are sipped. The food remains untouched. The yellow glare of the pears makes the eye ache.

'Surely the answer is in finding a place for the subjects, not in disbanding the Order itself.' Brother Alfred places his hands together on the table, his eyes scanning the room. 'If they cannot live here with us, can we not just send them off? To Edinburgh? London? Somewhere? Who would know? Our responsibilities ended. We have done all we can. We must leave this in God's hands. We must. Truly we must. To disband the Order is unnecessary.'

'As I have said, the matter of the Order has already been decided.' Bishop Constantine's rare flower had faded and irritation creeps into his voice.

'Tonight we are left with options two and three.'

Brother Roy starts calling up files on his computer. 'Alfred, my friend, I do not believe your suggestion can work, as much as it would be my greatest wish as well. The subjects have not been, shall we say, adjusted to the social environment. Educated, of course, in our best traditions, in so far as this was possible. Look here, the liturgy, classes in history, literature, art, science. I personally taught them mathematics and computer sciences, all those who came of school age, that is. But this does not make them prepared for life outside the Order. They are eighteen. Impetuous and full of naivete and hormones. They are normal young men. They would need socialisation, education in culture. This is a long process. Some say it is impossible unless started in the early years, the first five.'

'I cannot agree. Send them out, only let it be further away.

Send them to the Continent. Rome can arrange for identity papers, employment, housing. After that let the Almighty determine their fate. That is just. We should never have allowed the Order to be drawn into this entire affair. It has been a scandalous misadventure. Worse. A sin. A sin in the name of the Father, the Son and the Holy Ghost. A sin in the name of the Son. The Son, my brothers. The Son.' Brother Duncan's spit dances through the air and lands on the table. He moves his black sheathed arm forward and wipes away the wet. Silence overtakes him.

Father Roy begins quietly. 'To consider this realistically we must discuss the individual subjects. With the greatest respect to brothers Alfred and Duncan . . .'

'You can add my voice to theirs.' Brother Antonio calls from the end of the table.

'And mine as well. It is the only acceptable solution. Option two.' Edgar adds as he pushes the food tray away.

'Is it truly acceptable, reasonable, to inflict these men . . . indeed, can we call them "men" . . . to inflict these subjects on society? I misspoke when I called them "normal". We are all aware that we have seen much evidence to the contrary. J2, as we call him, "James", James appears to function in the most consistent manner, though as we know he is a quiet man, inclined to contemplation, coupled with occasional bursts of insight on the most astonishing matters. And not all of a rational nature, in my view. He manifests a deep knowledge of the liturgy, and curiously, all world religions. The latter were not included in detail in his education here. I can only assume he has been reading on his own in the library. Still he is a strange character, you would all agree. His spirit dances, true enough. But he is not a normal man. He cannot be released, not when we are uncertain as to his real nature. And the others, Bishop Constantine, you would support me here, there are serious questions about their suitability for life on the outside.'

'Unfortunately, the other two have evidenced deviant behaviour on numerous occasions. I need not remind you of the disappearance of the gold cross from the altar. We have every evidence that it was, J9, "David" as we refer to him, who took this irreplaceable and holy piece. And were it only that. Each of you, almost to the man, have had small and large items of your personal belongings disappear. None of these have ever been found, despite extensive searches of the buildings and grounds. This demonstrates not only the dishonesty of a common thief, but cunning as well. A dangerous combination.' Bishop Constantine opens the leather-bound book in front of him and flips through the pages. 'You will recall that there were several others who evidenced such criminal behaviour. J5 and J8 are the ones that come to readily to mind. And of the women, M10, M11 and M13 demonstrated either dishonest or seriously disruptive behaviour and in the case of the latter, definite promiscuous tendencies as she passed into the years of puberty. Unfortunately we did not have the opportunity to observe their full development, but as we all sadly know, there was nothing to confirm the hoped-for results. The others were too young when they died and it was impossible to make any significant determinations. M13 looked rather promising at first.'

'Yes, as a child her face was alight, was it not? Her cheeks shone, like the inside of a shell brought from the sea's shore.

I recall her with the greatest fondness. Of all those who died it was her that we all mourned the most.' Brother Antonio shook his head from side to side. 'The smallness of her hands, her coffin.'

'May I remind the group that we need to press on as the hour is late and we are some way from a decision.' Father Roy calls up a new file on his computer with the voice command, 'Cormac'. 'To continue with the thoughts of Bishop Constantine, there is Cormac, who, and I do not think I exaggerate here, is as thick as a tree trunk, as his name implies. I cannot see how he would function outside the Order. What employment would suit him? Cleaning latrines as he does here? And even at that we must remind him daily of his tasks, as if each morning were his first on this earth. Why, he cannot even read with any consistency, despite our greatest efforts. No, brothers, it would be an act of neither kindness nor justice to release this man.'

'Some material must have been disturbed during the initial replication procedures. Either that or he was like this in another life. A stupid man. That is possible. Of one thing we can be certain, that relic from the south of France is as much a fraud as Cormac is a foolish man! That much at least we know!' A voice from the right side of the table. Laughing.

'An idiot possibly. We can only hope that the relevant authorities in possession of this relic have been informed. What was the material? Bone? Blood?' Roy searches the file, then closes the cover on his computer. 'We must discuss option three.'

'I refuse. It is a sin. To even discuss this matter is a sin.' Brother Duncan's spit shines on the table again.

'They are not like other men. We have been through this debate before.'

'I did not agree with that point of view in the first debate and I cannot agree with it now. What is a man? They live and breathe. They have names. *We* gave them names. They weep. They laugh. They eat. Their bodies cleanse themselves. They sin and they repent. What is a man, if not this?' Duncan's sleeve becomes wetter and wetter as he rubs his forearms, first one and then the other, across the table to wipe up the evidence of his rage. 'If they are not men then I relinquish my right to the title as well. If forced to debate this question again, I am no longer a man but a monster.'

A brown winged moth from the walnuts lands on Brother Roy's clothing without his notice.

Silence gathers and falls away. The wild roses outside the window scrape the stone facade of the building as the wind moves them in the night. Bishop Constantine forms words and speaks. 'Brother Duncan, we are all in pain over this matter. I can confess to you that there have been many nights when I have lain awake, my thoughts running over events of the past eighteen, no, nineteen years. I am old. Yet I can still recall it, as if I were there today, my initial discussions with the Cardinal. We were both in the best years of our careers. You have to understand, there were exciting new technological and scientific advances that made all things seem possible. The Cardinal and I, both with scientific training, understood with a deep clarity, the implications of these developments, for both doctrine and practice. As men of the Church we had hesitations. But as men of science, we were, well . . . seduced. Enchanted.'

'Bishop, you are adrift.' A snort escapes Roy's breath. 'The decision to proceed with the project concerned the protection of the authority of the Church. It was about the relics. It was about confirming evidence. Using the new science to further Holy aims. In the service of the congregation. In the service of the Church. And yes, it was about placing ourselves closer to God. New horizons, not only those of the Church, but of mankind. It was a dream of hope for the future. To find Him. To meet the Son of God again. What greater goal? What greater good?'

Brother Duncan's words begin to froth forward again, robust and wet. 'You romanticise, Father Roy. It was about stealing the cloak of God. Who needed to know if the relics were real or not? They served their function, some of them for almost for two millennia. Why, in 2005, did we suddenly decide we needed to authenticate them? Gathering bits of cloth and tooth and bone from Italy and France, the Holy Land. To bring them here, to this place. Hidden away from the world in the dark Scottish forests. Crypts and vessels and vases and boxes, all standing empty, while believers continued to lay their prayers at the foot of barren altars. What of those prayers?' Duncan stands and paces the room. To one end of the table, then the other. To the window. Back to the table. His hands fly upwards and sideways. His body flaps. 'As for recreation . . .' The flapping of Duncan cannot be contained.

'What of them? If the relics were false, what of them then?' Father Roy spits back. He lifts his arms into the air joining Brother Duncan's dance, and in doing so frightens away the brown moth on his sleeve.

'If prayers were answered it was because of faith, not flesh nor bone.' Bishop Constantine looks towards the windows as the quietness of his robe gathers around his body. 'The reason for the project was that the new science made it possible. The knowledge, the best knowledge, existed here in Scotland. Others knew, but we knew the most. The procedures had been banned in America and elsewhere, so the relics were sent here. That was the only reason. We did not think it through. We were incapable of doing so.' Bishop Constantine sighs. 'To look into the eyes of God, through his Son. We were not capable of thought on this matter. Our ideas, our analysis, our imagination ended with replication. We could not, still cannot, judge the meaning.'

'But he is here.'

'He is not here. Can man make what rests in God's imagination? He is not here. It is only his shadow. A brother of a certain kind perhaps. But not the Son himself.'

'I agree. James is not the Son. The subjects, they are not men. They are duplicates. Need I *say* this? Therefore it is not a sin, against God, nor man to proceed with option three. I suggest that if we cannot move forward with a consensus, as clearly we cannot, we proceed with a vote. The hour is late. We are aware of the issues.' Father Roy throws his glare in the face of Brother Duncan who finally seats himself.

'A vote.'

'Yes, to the vote.'

'By a show of hands? Can we agree?' Twelve hands signal agreement.

'Bishop Constantine, may I? One question about option

three, before we proceed.' A voice from the left side of the table.

'Yes?'

'What method is to be used?'

'Injection. The same as with all the rest. I refer to those who did not succumb themselves. The same method used with those who deteriorated to a vegetative or subhuman state. The same. As for the time, it will take place immediately. Tomorrow. Any further questions?'

In answer to the silence Bishop Constantine proceeds. 'Those in favour of option two, please raise your right hand.' Constantine moves his hand upwards through the damp air. Five other hands follow. Brother Duncan. Brother Antonio. Brother Alfred. Brother Edgar. Brother Malcolm. 'I see. There is no need to call for the next option. We are at an unanticipated stalemate.'

'Call it anyway.' Duncan spits. 'Call it! Make those who have been silent, those who have said so little, those who have said too much, *make them say it*. Option three. Vote.' He turns towards the end of the table and watches Father Roy raise his moth dusted arm into the air. Five others follow in his shadow.

'I did not anticipate this result. We cannot move forward without a decision.' Constantine's shoulders fall into the night.

Duncan is on his feet again. 'Call them in. Call the subjects in. It is their fate. It is only just. Let them vote.' A din echoes off the stone walls.

The Bishop lifts his hands to cover his ears, then smooths back his hair, in one slow motion. 'Silence. Silence! Brothers,

Father Roy. Contain yourselves!' The silence moves around the room once again, touching each man on the back of the neck. 'Call them in.'

'Impossible! You expect them to vote on their own execution!' Father Roy roars.

'Call them in. Sit, Father Roy. Sit or you will be removed and your vote made void. Sit.' Bishop Constantine motions to Edgar to leave the room and summon the subjects. Moments as long as days pass. Time is stolen. An hour? Half? It is impossible to say.

Cold coffee is poured into empty cups and the last drops of whisky distributed. Roy takes a pear and rips at the yellow flesh with his teeth. Sweet juice gathers around the corners of his mouth, runs down his wrist, into his sleeve. He does not notice the dampness. He finishes and walks to the window, opens the shutter, and throws the core down into the darkness. There is no sound as it hits the ground below.

The door opens and Brother Edgar enters, followed by James, David, and Cormac. Their clothes are dense with the smell of the night air. Cormac stumbles. His shoes are large and unwieldy. His hands are slabs of flesh. He does not know where to put them. His eyes look intently at the stones on the floor. David tucks his half hanging shirt into his trousers. He stands up straight. He smooths his hair. Looks quickly at the mud on the soles of his shoes. His eyes graze the room, the face of each man.

Brother Edgar's eyes inspect the room as well. 'There are no chairs. Where shall they sit?'

'We will stand. We have been taking some exercise. Walking in the garden. Listening to the sounds of the night.

Cormac wished to hear stories about the stars again. We will stand.' James speaks in a quiet voice. It is the sound of water moving over smooth stones. 'We understand there is a decision to be made.' He stands in front of the table, David and Cormac on either side of him. He places his hands in his jeans. His white T-shirt is too large and hangs off his body. His brown hair is cropped short.

'The others are informed?' the Bishop inquires, looking into the eyes of James, trying to determine if they are blue or brown, the light of the stone room and the dim night masking their colour.

'They are aware, yes. We have discussed option two and option three, as you have called them. Brother Edgar told us the details of your discussions.'

'To the vote then,' the Bishop calls. 'I will ask you, man by man, what is your answer. Who will begin?'

'Your excellency, Bishop Constantine, let my vote come first. I have made mistakes, I know that. I repent. I ask your forgiveness. I will return what I have stolen. What I have sold, I will work for. I will give back each and every pound I have taken. Governors. Excellencies. Please. I will study the teachings. I will become one of you. Brothers. If you will let me . . .'

'David, man, this is not a reckoning. You have a vote. Use it or it will be taken away.' Bishop Constantine looks at his watch.

'Option two. It's the only one, isn't it? Option two. Please brothers. Please.' David falls on his knees, hands clasped. James leans down to help him to his feet again. David's body shakes as James lets go of his arm.

'Cormac?'

'I am not a happy man, yeah. I beg the pardon of you kind and generous brothers, and you there, Father, and you, your most honouring Bishop Constantine. It is no fault of yours, but I am a miserable man. Each pond I look into, each glass, each mirror, I see no reflection of my life. I don't know why, yeah. You think me stupid, but I am not. It is only that I can't see myself, yeah? I don't know why I am in this place. In my dreams I see a good place, but when I wake up, yeah, I am here.' His big hands move into the air grasping at something he sees. 'So I vote, yeah, for option three.'

Father Roy sits upright. 'Last vote! Last vote!'

James begins to speak. 'Roy, you misheard me in the confession box.'

'I did not ask you a question. Give us your vote.' Roy orders from the end of the table.

James continues. 'You misheard me in the confession box. My words were, "Forgive them Father for they have sinned." The thieves, Roy. I was referring to my friends, the thief and the fool, who are here before you. The ones who you seek to condemn. I asked the Father, the Father, not you, for forgiveness. Forgiveness for all the thieves and fools, and rogues, and men of dishonest character, and betrayers of the common character like yourself. Forgiveness for those who would lay bare, and twist, the light of nature. Forgiveness for those whose light has been twisted through no fault of their own. They know not what they do. You did not hear those words, Roy. But I said them then. You know them well.'

'Get him out of here! NOW! Get that man out of here!!!' Roy's black robe slides on the floor as he falls in the rush to push the bearded man with the short cropped hair out of the room.

'The last vote. Let us have the last vote!' Bishop Constantine bellows, a large voice somehow escaping his thin chest.

'My vote is clear.' James stands, still facing the table. 'Option three. The result is of no consequence.'

STEVE LEIGHTON
By Weary Well

I am not a bad man, although, to be sure, I am no saint.
Lust, greed, selfishness, cowardice, sloth, even arrogance and
impatience – all these sins do I readily admit to, as my story
will tell. I have fought against them as valiantly as the next
man and, like him, I have usually lost the fight. But murder?
Child abuse? Deceit? I cannot accept that I have committed
these acts although I have spent half my life plagued by the
thought that, in my indolent and impulsive youth, I was guilty
of them all. It is time that I told the truth about what happened
during those few strange days by Weary Well, a truth that only
I can tell – I and a woman who can speak but a single word.
Yes, after twenty years of uneasy denial, it's time I set the
record straight – for my own peace of mind, if for no more
noble reason.

I was, as befits the name, exhausted and aflame with thirst
when first I came upon the Weary Well. After days of trudging
across wild moors and barren heathlands, the valley seemed
like Paradise – meadows jewelled with poppies and buttercups,
orchards smothered in blossom, fat-uddered cows grazing in
the afternoon sun. Sheltered in a copse of oaks stood the

carpenter's cottage, a barn and workshed and, a little way off, the welcome sight of the rough stone wall of Weary Well.

I ran down from the hillside, the lure of water overcoming any caution I would normally have felt upon encountering the haunts of men after so many days of solitary roaming. A pail attached to a rusty chain sat upon the rim of the well. I threw it down into the deep blackness, heard the splash then pulled and pulled until that glistening nectar emerged, cool and clear, the wine of God. I poured it into my eagerly open throat, sighed my pleasure then poured some more. Ecstasy – the taste of water to a thirsty man!

'Water is free to any traveller,' came a voice behind me. 'Food will cost you a few hours' work.'

I turned to look into the face of the carpenter, a short man with bulging arms and massive hands, laughing blue eyes and a smile that was as welcoming as the water from his well.

We worked together in the woods till the sun had set, sawing planks of oak and ash and dragging them to the shed by the cottage, strenuous work relieved only by frequent draughts from that marvellous well. We spoke little, both of us men of few words, but I told him, as we supped from the pail, of my roving life, of days spent walking from village to village, following the harvest or any other work that came my way, of nights beneath the holy awning with only the stars for company.

He told me of a different life, a life of sparse adventure, perhaps, but one bathed in contentment and the security of home. Never had he ventured more than a dozen miles from the cottage of his birth. The crafting of wood into beautiful furniture was both his purpose and his joy. Once, he told me, he had loved a wife but death had taken her and now his daughter was his one companion.

I met her when we packed away our tools and plodded wearily back to the cottage for supper. No more than fourteen summers old, she was coy yet keen to snatch a frequent glance at me, as gangling as her father was robust, her face almost pretty when it peered out from within the drapes of her matted, blonde hair. Her hands were dainty and graceful as she ladled out our soup and cut our bread.

Her name was Placebo – the strangest name I've ever heard. 'I shall please' – and please she did. The carpenter told me that she'd spoken no words since her mother died, no words, that is, save 'Yes.'

She blushed at this and hid her face from mine amidst her curling locks.

'Is this true?' I asked, wishing to entice her into conversation.

'Yes,' she whispered.

'Can't say no,' her father told me with a peculiarly unfatherly wink and I, who had lived without the touch of a woman's flesh for far too long, began to feel the stirrings of desire.

He plied me with mead, glad, no doubt, of some more loquacious company than his daughter could offer, and insisted that I should stay the night. I did not gainsay him and he showed me to an attic room, clean but empty of all but a mat upon the boards, a stool and a huge bed, its ends and posts carved with the smooth, swirling patterns that were the mark of his craftsmanship. I flopped onto the mattress, blew out my candle and was asleep at once.

I awoke to a touch upon my unshaven cheek. Moonlight

was pouring through a high, narrow window above me, shimmering on Placebo's tangled locks, her moist eyes – no longer coy but wide with longing – her naked breasts which I, bereft of any thoughts of propriety in my hypnagogic state, reached up and cupped in my hands. She lowered her body onto mine.

'Yes,' she murmured.

What could I do? What would any man do? Before I knew it, my hands were gripping her buttocks, my lips pressed against hers, my desire burning like a forest fire. She writhed and sighed on top of me as I thrust into her, harder and harder, with the same urgency and delight as I had felt earlier that day, quaffing water from the Weary Well.

I present no excuses for my behaviour, other than suggesting that I was infected by the unstoppable momentum of lust. It shames me, now, that I should have so abused the hospitality of the carpenter. But then, in the bed he had fashioned so lovingly, I gave him not a single thought. I was aware of nothing but the wonder of Placebo's young body, offered with such unexpected and unrequested benevolence as I had never before, nor since, experienced. I confess that I was powerless to resist.

But, in the fury of our passion, the bed began to creak and groan, its legs banging against the floorboards. And then, as we reached the zenith of our lust and relaxed into the afterglow, the door burst open. There stood the carpenter in his nightshirt, a candle in his hand and a look upon his reddened face that any father can well imagine.

He said nothing, just glared, his eyes, it seemed to me, about to explode from their sockets. Placebo leapt from my body and scampered past him out the room. As for me, I just lay there on my back, fully prepared to take whatever punishment the carpenter cared to mete. No doubt I was prepared to die. I would not have argued or resisted. I had no defence. Perhaps I even thought that death was fair recompense for those few minutes of blissful abandon.

For what the carpenter did next, I can offer no explanation, no hint of his possible motive. He turned his back on me, left the room and slammed the door behind him. A few minutes later, as I lay there still, not knowing whether to feel relieved or fearful, I heard a banging outside the wooden door, the banging of hammer on nails that went on and on, a hundred times or more. I knew, without considering the consequences, exactly what was happening. Half a dozen sturdy planks nailed across the door frame with all the permanence of the carpenter's skill. I was sealed up within the room of my undoing. I looked up to the tiny, slit-like window, high on the wall behind me, through which a beam of moonlight still streamed. Its width would barely take an arm, never an entire body. I was trapped. This was to be my tomb, this wondrous bed my coffin.

Presumably I slept – sleep has always been my great escape – for the next thing I knew was daylight bathing the room in a glow of seeming normality and, once more, a burning thirst within my throat. I quickly recalled the events of the night and turned my mind to escape. The window was, indeed, no option and the door as firmly secured as a steel cage. I tried shouting until I was hoarse but no sound responded to my cries either from within the cottage or beyond. I sat upon the bed and contemplated my fate. What was I to do?

Nothing, it seemed, but wait. My fate was in the hands of the carpenter and I had no clue as to his intentions. He had appeared, the previous day, to be a friendly and a Christian man, but, knowing nothing of the emotions of fatherhood, how could I predict his reaction to my shameful abuse of his beloved daughter?

And so I waited, alone with my thoughts and self-recriminations, cocooned in my cell with even my luxurious bed now a sour comfort. For two days I waited, driven wild by boredom and fear, by regret and dreams of freedom, by, above all, a thirst that seemed to be sucking the life from me, a torture more painful than anything the carpenter could have devised for me. Or perhaps this was his torture?

On the third day, I was stirred from a crazed reverie by a knocking on the floorboards. I hastily removed the mat, located the source of the sound and began struggling to lever up the boards.

'Yes,' came a muffled word of encouragement.

First I broke the nails of both my hands, then the blade of my penknife and the buckle of my belt, but the boards would not budge. I cursed the skill of the carpenter.

'Yes, yes, yes.' Placebo's voice urged me on.

Finally I managed to rip up a single board and then its neighbour. And there, beneath me, was the dusty face of my erstwhile temptress, staring up at me from the tiny channel between the solid oak beams that supported the upper part of the cottage.

She wriggled an arm through the hole in the boards, I took it and pulled and she gradually eased herself into the room. She flung her arms around my neck and tried to hug me but

I pushed her away. Pleased though I was to see her, I had no wish to do anything more to incur her father's wrath.

She pointed hopefully to the bed. 'Yes?'

'No. Definitely not. Not now. Must get out of here,' I managed to say. My mouth was as dry as stone and I had trouble speaking. We were a fine pair – she with only one word to say and I barely able to articulate any. 'Water. You have any water?'

She shook her head. Suddenly I had an idea, grabbed her face between my hands and kissed her. As her mouth opened to meet mine, I sucked at her saliva. It was only a drop, but enough to wet my lips. Unfortunately, though, she took it as a preliminary to further intimacy and started guiding me towards the bed. God, the girl was insatiable but I was most definitely not in the mood!

I think she finally got the message of my reluctance and pointed at the gap in the floorboards. 'Yes?'

I examined the space between the beams dubiously. I am not a small man and the thought of ending up wedged in that dark and dusty tunnel seemed worse than remaining in my prison cell. But thirst is a powerful driving force. I would have tried anything.

'Yes,' Placebo decided, eagerly, and she flung herself to the floor and slithered into the gap. It was several minutes before her feet disappeared from view, which did not reassure me.

'Yes, yes.' I heard her distant voice urging me to follow.

So began an hour of agony and near desperation. To this day, I don't know how I managed it, but somehow I inched my way through the tiny space between floorboards and downstairs ceiling, choking on the dry dust, elbows, shoulders, hips and knees rubbed red raw by the rough wood, ribs crushed so tight that I could barely breathe. I suppose it was no longer than six feet but it seemed interminable and, at times, I thought I was completely jammed and would surely break a bone if I forced myself any further. But the light streaming in from Placebo's room, next to my barricaded door, where she had removed a couple of floorboards, goaded me onwards. Finally I emerged, bruised and battered but free at last.

Now she grabbed my hand and pointed at her own bed in the corner of the room. 'Yes?'

'No!' I shouted, angrily. I knew that she had just saved my life but I could not forget that it was her carnal craving for my body that had initiated this sad affair in the first place. I tried to calm myself. 'First, I need water.'

She shook her head.

'The well!' The image, as it sprang into my mind, was like a vision of heaven.

'Yes, yes!'

I ran from the room, hurtled down the stairs and through the cottage door. I was charging down the slope towards Weary Well, too late to take precautions, before I saw the carpenter.

He was sitting on the low stone wall of the well, lifting the pail of freshly drawn, cool, clear water to his lips. It was a hot, sunny day – I hadn't noticed – and he was taking a break from his labours.

I rushed on, careless of the consequences, grabbed the pail from his hands and poured that beautiful water into my gaping mouth.

Perhaps my sudden arrival startled him and upset his

balance. Perhaps I pushed him in my eagerness to quench my burning thirst – I just don't know. As I gulped down mouthful after mouthful, I watched him slowly topple over backwards and fall, head first, into the depths of Weary Well.

The splash, some seconds later, brought me to my senses. I peered into the blackness. Nothing. I thrust my head as far into the gaping pit as I dared and strained my ears. Not a sound. I flung the pail in, its chain securely fixed to the outer wall of the well, scrambled over the wall and clambered down, clinging to the chain and finding ample footholds amongst the rough stones. Thirty feet or more down, my feet hit the water. I looked up at a glowing, pure blue disc of sky, high above me. Then, as my eyes grew accustomed to the darkness, I saw two big boots breaking the surface of the water, as still as death. I lowered myself to waist depth and reached out, only to discover that the carpenter's body was firmly wedged into a constriction at the base of the well. Pull as I might, I couldn't budge him.

By this time, his head had been submerged for a good five minutes and the absence of all movement convinced me of the finality of his state. Whether he had drowned or smashed his head on the well floor, I couldn't tell. And nor did I much care. Panic seized me and I hauled myself, hand over hand, up the chain and tumbled over the wall into the land of the living.

Without thinking, I pulled the pail back up, desperate for more water, but when I raised it to my lips, I saw, with horror, that it was clear no more. Clouds of blood swirled around in it, deep red, polluted with the vital fluid of the carpenter.

I ran – into the woods and away from that place. For hours I ran until I came upon a stream and washed away the taste of blood and fear and, I hoped in vain, the memories of my fateful impetuosity. Then, as darkness fell, I slunk into a thicket and spent a restless night with the creatures of the forest floor.

No, I did not return – and that shameful fact has tormented me more than anything. How could I have left Placebo to discover for herself, as she surely would, the horror of her father's death? How could I not claim responsibility for my part in his gruesome end? How could I blot from my mind the whole strange and sorry business? Because I am a coward, of course, although I pretend to myself that it is because I am a survivor, and always have been. No, I am not proud of the fact. I despise myself.

Some six months later, I happened upon the vicinity of the Weary Well once more. I befriended a man in the local tavern and, over our pints, I brought up the subject.

'I once knew the carpenter who lives in the cottage by the well,' I remarked, all innocently. 'What's become of him, d'you know?'

He told me the tale. Many days after my hasty departure, apparently, the carpenter's body was discovered in the blood-red water of the well. It needed a rope and horse to winch him out. Within the cottage, the men of the village, searching for Placebo, came across my boarded up door. Eventually, for the carpenter, of course, had done a thorough job, they broke into the room and there found Placebo, lying naked and shaking with fright on that bed on which we had once shared our lust.

'What had happened?' I asked my companion with feigned curiosity.

'Who knows?' he replied. 'The girl is a simpleton, and a mute, to boot. "Yes" is the only word she ever speaks. "Yes" to everything she is asked. No one could get any sense from her, neither concerning how she came to be sealed in that room nor how her father had died.'

I knew both, though I said nothing. She must have crawled back through that tiny passageway, pulling the boards in her room back into place as she went then replacing the boards and mat in my room to conceal all trace of her entry. The reason why was the one thing that eluded me. But Placebo, as I knew full well, was not one to whom normal motives could be ascribed.

'She was taken in by some local worthies,' my drinking companion continued, 'and, some months later, it emerged that she was pregnant. Now, what d'you make of that, my friend?'

I shook my head, stunned into silence.

'Course, then we understood what had happened. The carpenter, without the comfort of a woman's love for years, had defiled his own daughter. Shamed by what he had done, we can but presume, he had sealed her forever in the room in which he had perpetrated the vile deed and taken his own life in the depths of the well.'

And that, in essence, became the legend of Weary Well. No third party was ever sought, no suggestion that a fugitive from justice – as I imagined myself to be – had fertilised the girl and murdered or, at least, hastened the demise of her father. The only sullied reputation was his and he had atoned for his sin in the only honourable way. The tale was concluded, the legend assigned to local folklore.

But did it ease my conscience? I confess that it did not. And yet I wound my way, that day, with a lighter step and set out upon the rest of my life.

Twenty years past and I found myself, again, at the cottage by Weary Well, my guise concealed by baldness, a greying beard and the scars of many adventures. Placebo lived there still, a grown woman, now – she didn't recognise me but I did her, of course – and with her lived her son, himself a carpenter, tall and stout. Takes after his father, they no doubt said in the village (or after his grandfather, perhaps), but I knew better. He had the look of a rover about him. And did I detect, in his eyes, the look of a coward?

I gave nothing away. How could I? Perhaps I felt a twinge of paternal pride but, with customary insensitivity, I denied it.

I asked Placebo if I might take a drink of water from the well and she smiled, a long-forgotten, well-remembered smile. 'Yes,' she said.

As, with scant regard for troubled memories, I tossed the pail into the depths of Weary Well, I became aware of activity around the cottage, of voices in the workshed and children's laughter in the parlour.

'How many children do you have?' I asked.

She raised her dainty hand and spreads out the fingers.

'Five?'

'Yes.'

So Placebo – I shall please – had done her share of pleasing over the years.

'And your husband?'

She shook her head, her eyes downcast, a flush beginning

on her still smooth and youthful cheeks. She was as bashful as she had been when first I saw her, twenty years before.

So why had I returned? Was it sheer curiosity? Or did I seek to somehow atone for my former sins? If God is the only forgiver of sins, then I await the time when I stand before Him. But it was God who made me as I am, and bade me act the way I did. I do not believe, as the preachers say, that He who makes the heavenly spheres revolve upon their perfect way and causes the flower bud to unfurl when the season is ripe should allow any less control in the lives of men. No, it is not God from whom we should seek forgiveness, but those souls whose lives we hurt by our hasty deeds.

'Do you remember me?' I asked Placebo.

She glanced up for just a moment but I could see the dawn of recognition in her eyes. She nodded her head as her flush deepened, and I wondered how she had thought of me over those long years. Had I wronged her? Or had we both just done what our natures and the wiles of circumstance dictated?

'And do you forgive me?' I asked, knowing the only answer she could give.

'Yes,' she said.

ADAM LLOYD-BAKER
Small Change

First coffee of the day amongst rolled posters and film stars sheathed in bubblewrap. I am joined by Marvin. We hate our jobs, hate our boss, and that, I suppose, makes us friends.

Marvin sits on a stack of film cans. He unpacks his bag: sandwiches, banana, book.

'There's a rumour,' says Marvin.

'There's always a rumour.'

'They say you're putting in for management.'

'Between you and me, yeah.'

'What the hell for?'

'They made a rule. All staff have to wear the uniform. Projectionists included. My thirtieth birthday is coming up. If, on that day, I'm wearing do-you-want-fries-with-that corporate pyjamas I will have a serious crisis about the direction my life has taken.'

'Will you still talk to me when you're a suit?'

'I haven't got the job yet.'

* * *

There are no windows in the cinema. It is a capsule of retail architecture: curves and chrome and artificial light. A sense of dislocation as you step over the threshold. You are leaving your town and are entering an international leisure zone, like shopping malls or the purlieu of airports.

The morning routine:

Start the boilers. Watch through a little window as the ignition chamber, carbon coated like a crematorium oven, is filled with fire.

Power up the cinema. Slap breakers to ON. AC hum. The hiss of extractor fans builds to an oceanic roar.

Banks of switches. The building comes to life like a fair-ground ride. The auditoria glow red like a desert sunset. Piped film scores evoke Romance, Trepidation, Run Like Hell.

Sometimes, when I am down in the tunnels with the heat and hum of the machines, my thoughts turn sad. I am overcome by nostalgia and regret. Fleeting sensations from my backbrain: gull caws and breaking waves, rockpools and driftwood, a child's delight in seashells. I am engulfed in the viscous sepia of memory, like a bug caught in amber. Nights like these I don't want to be alone. I prowl the auditoria and watch movies that end in a fireball and a kiss.

Sometimes I fall in love with girls on the screen. I watch her everyday, a pretty girl in the LA sun, and she smiles and becomes my friend. And when the film has finished its run, when it's time for her to be boxed and shipped, it's like waving goodbye on a station platform. I pack those tins as tenderly as I can, then laugh at myself because she was just coloured light.

I like the girls that work as usherettes. I listen to their talk but they don't have a second glance for a working man with a tool belt and toe-cap boots. For them, the cinema is an interlude between college and career. They work a few months then move on.

I have scabs on my knuckles, and fingernails I can't get clean no matter how hard I scrub. I have found my first grey hairs. Youth and beauty viewed through a closing door.

I wish I were better with tools. When I buy sandwiches at Franco's across the street I feel intimidated by the plumbers and brickies sitting around me. I wear boots and a tool belt. I pretend the heat and noise of the projection box is foundry work, that my life is a Bruce Springsteen song, but these guys are the real thing.

The construction workers are sexually intimidating. I have a catalogue of pornographic videos and the gay section is full of men in hard hats and overalls.

'SEYMOUR BUTTS PRESENTS: MR FIX IT' (G364)
'Get ready to work with the men of the Mr Fix It Construction Co. This crew is fully equipped to handle your job. When every-thing explodes into an orgy of men, shopfloor sweat and Ken Rykers 10" powertool you'll be glad you called Mr Fix It!'
'FULL SERVICE 2: SWEATING GREASE' (G937)
'There's more than petrol pouring out at the pumps! Watch as Ben Masters and his mechanic buddies save their gas station from bankruptcy with hot, hard, man to man sex. Fill up with the hottest, hardest studs around.'

I saw an office worker park next to the building site up the street. The workmen shouted from the scaffolding, called him a fat bastard. The man locked his car and hurried away blushing like a woman.

The only physical engagement most guys have with their work is keyboard RSI.

I have been a projectionist five years. Each day is the same as the last. In the morning I bring heat and light to the auditoria, and fix what is broken. In the evening I run films. Nothing changes, except I used to be twenty-five and now I am thirty.

* * *

Each time I am called to Townsend's study it is like a summons to the headmaster's study. The voice on the radio, impassive like Mission Control:

'Spence, meet me in the office right away.'

Immediately I feel anxious and ashamed.

I think about school a lot. Something lacking in the boys I knew. They got stuck halfway to adulthood. They work in call-centres and bars. None of us married. All of us rent.

Townsend keeps me waiting. It's a power thing, puts me on the backfoot. I knock once, knock twice. I picture him behind the door counting to thirty. His waking hours are a carefully honed mindfuck.

'Come in.'

Townsend's first act as manager was to order new filing cabinets and a bigger desk. Depressions in the carpet map how the room used to be.

'I have a uniform for you,' he says. 'Large, extra large. See what fits.'

The uniform is a blue tracksuit with matching baseball cap.

'This is polyester,' I say. 'We get a lot of static in the projection box. I wore a polyester shirt to work once and my hair bushed out like an Afro. Anyone who shook hands with me got third-degree burns.'

I had rehearsed this confrontation during the afternoon. In my daydream I was lucid and wise.

'The uniform was designed for ticketbooth women,' I said, pacing the projection box, lecturing an empty chair. 'It was not intended to be worn by technicians. I can't climb ladders and crawl through ceiling voids in a sweat top. It's emasculating to be dressed the same as girls in the kiosk.'

Townsend melted before my reason and I left him, sitting at his desk, a humbled man.

'I appreciate your concerns,' says Townsend, which means Fuck You. 'Even so I have to ask you to wear the uniform. Some of the ladies don't like the baseball caps. In fact Mrs Prufock is drawing up a petition. You see I can't start making exceptions.'

'The projection booth is hotter than hell. It reaches ninety degrees in summer.'

'By all means take off your sweatshirt when you're in the box. But while you are in the lobby you really ought to wear the uniform.'

If I could press a button to give him cancer, I would.

* * *

The cinema used to be a theatre. My den is backstage.

The petty thrill of officialdom: a big bunch of keys and the right to push through doors marked No Entry.

My den is an old dressing room. It contains an armchair, a television, and a kettle. There is a make-up table and gilt mirror. Rotting grandeur. Music hall razzle-dazzle mouldering in Haversham twilight.

I wipe grime from the mirror. I look ridiculous in the uniform. I look like a Mongoloid janitor.

* * *

'I can't lie to you,' says Marvin. 'You look like a retard.'

I am fixing a cubicle lock in the ladies' lavatory. A faint sexual thrill to be trespassing on exclusively female territory. The washstand mirrors show how big my arse looks in the new uniform.

'Re-branding,' says Marvin. 'Makes you feel like cattle, doesn't it?'

'I have two days off. I'm going to buy a bottle and not have a coherent thought till Monday.'

'Have you ever played poker?'

'No.'

'I was thinking of getting a poker school together. Make it a regular thing. Play for pennies, nothing heavy.'

'Asked anyone else?'

'Only thought of it this afternoon.'

'I wanted to get a Dungeons and Dragons game going. This was years back. I wanted to get a game going and make it a weekend thing. No one interested. Total apathy. This myth you're supposed to have a bunch of friends and go through life together, lean on each other down the years. Nobody lives like that. Five senses: that's all you've got.'

'Are you up for this or not?'

'If you can make it happen, then what the fuck.'

Marvin sits on the washstand.

'There's a car boot sale on Wednesday. At the playing field.'

'What do you need?'

'Forties, sixties. BC fixtures. Any fluorescent tubes.'

'Put your car round the back tonight. Make sure the cameras can't see you.'

I bet usherettes steal torch batteries. I bet Townsend steals stationery. We all leech off the company. We suck on it like a giant tit.

I twist four cross-head screws into the cubicle door.

'You know this job interview is a scam,' says Marvin. 'I've seen this kind of thing before. Places I've worked. Shops, supermarkets. Same deal.'

'Like what?'

'You've been here a while. I'm not telling you anything you didn't know already. Management like it when employees put in for promotion. Shows they have a motivated workforce. Doesn't mean there's a vacancy. They had some hot-shot lined up for this job all along.'

'Yeah,' I sigh and pack away my tools.

'You need a game plan. Otherwise it's minimum wage all your life.'

'Not that you want to see me fail or anything.'

'People like you and me: we know what it's like to be passed over. You shouldn't stand still for it. You shouldn't let them do it to you.'

'Don't worry. I got dreams.'

* * *

I try to steal something everyday. I give this company a big slice of lifetime so the way I look at it, they owe me. Okay: they pay me a wage, they don't ask me to work for free, but running films gets me a room and bad food. I live hand to mouth. Taking their money is ugly like charity, ugly like putting coins in an outstretched hand. I feel stepped on. Last week Townsend gave me a new dustpan and brush. He said: 'Let's make sure it doesn't get mixed up with the cleaner's stuff.' He bit the cap off a Magic Marker and wrote HANDYMAN on the brush. I am not a handyman. I am a Cinema Technician. That's my job description. I'd like to see him fix the air conditioning, the boiler, the projectors. I should walk out and let him be without his handyman. He'd be helpless. He'd be fucked.

I steal stuff from the supply store: light bulbs, parcel tape, pens, pencils, rubber bands, garbage bags. I slip something in my pocket each morning and feel better about Townsend's management bullshit: talk of setting key action performance core benchmarks, staff appraisal protocols with three-sixty-degree feedback procedures. I'd like to see the fucker change a plug. Anyway, I feel in control of my life if I go to the supply room, shake a couple of 3 amp fuses into my palm and put them in my pocket. A fuse is worth as much as a sheet of paper but I took it and now it is mine. If I get summoned to

Townsend's office and disciplined for putting a film on late I'm still in control because there is a fuse in my pocket and more like it at home. Sometimes I ball my coat to a pillow and sleep on the projection box floor. Sometimes I take a skipping rope from my locker and do a little gym routine in the dead time between films. It's important to have secrets. It's important to have your own agenda.

The cinema has no tangible stock. We sell dreams. Nothing I can hide under my coat and purloin. There are sweets on the pick 'n' mix stand but they guard those Jelly Babies like bullion. If I could get my hands on a couple of kilos of Cannibal Crocs, Spogs, Strawbz, Fruitettes or Candy Skulls, I could sell them. I could bag them up and sell them at car boot sales with Marvin. But it's just not possible to steal sweets in bulk. They keep track. They know exactly how many wholesale cartons are in the stock room, and they weigh the plastic display boxes each night. It's like marking a whisky bottle to make sure nobody raids your drinks cabinet. And the sweet stand is covered by CCTV cameras. That's how Claire got caught.

Claire stole money. Townsend noticed a shitload more sweets being consumed than paid for. He re-angled a CCTV camera to watch the kiosk girls. Claire was palming tenners. Taking the money and cancelling the sale. She got fired. I don't know if she was prosecuted. That kind of petty theft doesn't make the papers.

Claire was destined to be caught. You could tell. She was a loser and a klutz. Someone should have taken her aside. 'You have sad eyes and whatever you try in this life will fail.' One of those people who contracted failure young.

I could steal popcorn. We use so much no one keeps

track. As soon as we run out Townsend phones for another truckload.

The popcorn tastes like shit but we sell a dumpster load everyday so I guess the public never learn. The popcorn isn't fresh. It arrives pre-popped in weightless boxes the size of a phone booth. Inside the boxes are polythene sleeves filled with popcorn. For some reason, every time I see a kiosk girl teasing popcorn out of one of these sleeves, I am reminded of goldfish shit: the little back strings that used to hang out of my pet goldfish and trail behind him as he swam.

No one would know if I stole one of those big, wholesale boxes. Like I say, no one keeps track.

If I return to the building during the night I could take what I want and no one would stop me. All I need is the alarm code.

* * *

Gordon Street is a terrace rented room by room to students and social security claimants. Windows lit, throughout the night, by the cold light of television.

Home is the basement flat at Number Nine.

The pub has emptied and the kebab shop is filled with drunks. I buy a half bottle at One Stop and walk to the good end of town. The streets are slick with rain. The radio says if the sky clears we might see a comet.

Each Regency mews has an alleyway running behind it. I stand in the dark, sip from the bottle and watch the windows. Warm lights behind the blinds. Bathrooms misted up. Good families doing whatever good families do on a Friday night.

I spend each day doing a job I hate, same as my father and his father before him. That's the lineage. Down the centuries versions of me shovelled shit and hoped better things for his son. It ends here. I refuse to live like this anymore.

ANDREW LLOYD-JONES
Coveting

The first caller of the morning is calm, pleasant. It makes a change. Usually people call the main station before they get through to us, so by the time they get through, they can be pretty pissed off. But this one is calm. Like I say, pleasant.

Hello, I say. Marylebone Lost Property. Can I help you?

Uh, yes, he replies. I think I may have left a case on the train last night.

I see, I say. Can you give me the details? I bring out the green form from the racks beneath the desk. It's the one we use to note down the details of lost property.

Right, I say. What kind of case was it exactly?

Uh, well, it was average sized, I suppose, he begins. About half a metre long. Rectangular. Black.

Any handles? I ask.

Just the one, he says. On top. It looks a bit like an instrument case.

I know the kind of thing, I say. So there's an instrument in it?

No, he says. It's got a leg in it. A false leg.

I note it down. Prosthetic. I'm pretty sure I spell it

wrong, but I'm the only one who reads these things any-way.

Left or right? I ask out of idle curiosity more than anything else. It's not as if there's a place for it on the form or anything.

Left, he answers.

And where do you think you left it?

Uh, it was on the eleven thirty-two from Marylebone last night, he says.

A lot of people lose things on the eleven thirty-two. It's the pubs. But I'm surprised someone would get so drunk as to lose a leg, even if it was in a suitcase. I wonder if the man on the other end of the phone is wearing a false leg right now. Maybe it wasn't even his leg. Maybe he's a prosthetic salesman. Or a designer.

I'll just check the computer, I tell him. But it can take a couple days sometimes for things to turn up.

I tap the details of the train into the computer. A list of items comes up on the screen for items from that route. It's the usual stuff: three mobile phones, two umbrellas, one wallet, two jackets, two pairs of glasses, a pair of high heels, one Game Boy, but no case.

I tell him nothing matching the description of his case has been handed in yet, but that I'm sure it'll turn up. I tell him to try back in a couple of days, and he thanks me politely before hanging up.

* * *

I've been working in the lost property office at Baker Street for the past eight years. Usually, people I meet just want to know what the most expensive item I've ever found is. They talk about it like it's me who finds them personally. But it's not. The office has got more and more busy over the past few years. There's hardly any room anywhere. We used to have a staff lounge, but that's being used for Coats and Hats now.

I've found that you can pretty well tell how the economy's doing by how busy we are. When things are going well, people as a rule can't be bothered with your everyday lost items, like umbrellas, coats and so on. A few years ago, when things were a bit leaner, we hardly had a moment's peace. Everyone wanted everything back, and yesterday. People keep telling me, you should let the lads in the city know about that. You could predict the market with knowledge like that. I discussed it with once with Sal, my wife, but she thought I was joking. I didn't mention it again.

There are exceptions to the rule, too – things that people will come looking for, no matter how well off they are or how well the economy's doing. They can be the strangest things. Sometimes it's jewellery, sometimes they're items of clothing, sometimes they're Thermos flasks, but you can see the thing they have in common is that they're special for some reason. Sometimes the owners don't even know why. In which case I think they should be grateful for having lost them. And more grateful to us for giving them the chance to have them back.

I'd like to lose something that meant that much to me.

***

In the afternoon a man in a suit comes into the office. I look up, checking his legs as he walks towards the desk. I guess I've been examining everyone's legs since this morning.

I've lost my wallet, he says straight away.

He looks flustered, but I'm pretty certain those are his actual legs.

Okay, I reply. I just need to fill out some details, but he interrupts me before I get a chance to finish my sentence.

I don't care about the wallet or the money, he says. It's not the wallet I'm worried about. Or the cards. Or the money. You can keep the money. But there are some photos. In the wallet, of my son. They're the only ones I've got.

I can see there are tears in his eyes as he gives me the details. He was on the 7.02 into Marylebone from Gerrards Cross. He would have come sooner, but didn't notice his wallet was missing until lunchtime. Definitely had the wallet when he got onto the train, as he paid for his ticket with a ten-pound note. These aren't details I need for the form, but I can see he's upset, so I write them down anyway.

He gives me a description of the wallet (black, soft leather, credit card compartments and billfold) as well as one of his son (six years old, standing by a swimming pool wearing red trunks, and eight years old, wearing a brown school jumper and tie), which I carefully note down. The computer says nothing has been handed in, and I tell him I've been on since eight o'clock myself and haven't seen any wallets matching his description. But sometimes things get handed into the drivers, who don't always pass on lost property until they've finished their shift. It can take a couple of days.

So don't worry, I tell him. It's sure to turn up.

It's just the photos, he says again. Just the photos.

Even though I've already taken down his numbers (work, home and mobile), he hands me his card as he leaves. I thank him, and tell him I'll call personally as soon as I hear anything.

He walks out slower than he came, not looking flustered any more, just sad. The way he walks, as he leaves, it seems as though both his legs are made of wood.

* * *

On my lunch-break, I walk past a luggage shop. I must have passed it a thousand times, but I go in for a look. There's a selection of wallets in the window. Inside the shop, I take my own wallet out of my pocket. Sal gave it to me about ten years ago and it's getting a bit worn round the edges. I pick out a new one. It's a black, soft leather wallet, with credit card compartments as well as a billfold. It's more than I'd normally pay, but I buy it anyway. I show it to Sal that night.

What do you need a new wallet for? She's not impressed. What's wrong with the one you've got?

It's old, I say. And worn out.

It didn't look worn out to me, she replies.

Usually Sal loves to hear about the things people have lost, but I decide it's not a good time to tell her about the man and the photographs of the boy. So while she makes the tea, I move the contents of my old wallet into the new one. I like the way it smells. It makes the contents of my old wallet seem different.

I close my eyes and think about the boy until Sal comes in with the tea.

* * *

The next day, I take a call from a woman who cries down the phone at me. She left her address book (red cover, fake snakeskin, first address Beth Andrews) on the six twenty-nine to Amersham and was quite composed when she called. But when I tell her her address book has been handed in and is here at the office, she bursts into tears.

Oh, God, thank you, she says.

Uh. That's OK, I say. Things always turn up.

God, I don't know what I would have done if I'd lost it, she sniffs. It's got my whole life in it. Everyone.

Uh, I'm glad it's, uh, turned up, I say.

Oh God, she says, and starts crying again.

Eventually, she stops weeping for long enough to tell me she'll be in the following day to pick it up. She thanks me a few more times and puts the phone down.

I go to the racks and find the address book. It's quite full. She probably sends out a lot of Christmas cards. She might even send us one too, at the office. I've had that before. From the people we help. I don't really know what to call the people we deal with. One of the training manuals says they're called customers, but I can't see how. We don't sell them anything. We reunite them with the things they've lost. Like shepherds.

I've never had an address book as full as this one. I flick to the back of the book. I'm relieved to see she doesn't know anyone whose surname begins with an X. I've never heard of anyone whose surname begins with an X.

She doesn't know anyone whose surname begins with Q either.

I jump when one of the mobile phones starts to ring. We've got a box of them, about thirty at the minute. We're not supposed to interfere with them in any way, so they just go on ringing until the batteries die. We've tried covering them with old jackets, but you can still hear them. I slide the address book into an envelope and put it to one side.

* * *

That night I take the address book home with me. After Sal goes to bed, I take the phone into the kitchen and flick through the numbers. I select a local number from the D's, Jennifer Davies. There are two entries, one obviously for a mobile, but I pick the regular phone line. The phone rings twice before someone picks it up.

A voice at the other end of the line says, Hello?

It's a woman's voice. She sounds young. And like a brunette. I knew someone who sounded like her before I was married. She was a brunette.

Hello, I say. How are you?

There's a nervous laugh. Uh, fine, she says. Sorry, who is this?

This is Nick, I say. Nick Stevens.

There's a pause, and then she says, I'm sorry. Do I know you? I don't mean to be rude . . .

Uh, no, I'm sorry, I say. I think I've called the wrong number.

That's okay, she replies.

I hesitate before saying, Well, goodbye.

She gives the same nervous laugh. Bye then, she says.

There's a brief pause before the phone is rattled onto its plastic holder at the other end. I put the phone down and go into the kitchen to make some tea.

* * *

The next day I'm out front, writing down the details of the woman who lost her address book, when the door of the office opens and a woman walks in. She's maybe in her early thirties, but could be younger. She's wearing a blue denim jacket and black jeans, and has a bag slung across her shoulder. She reminds me of a girl I went out with for a while at college. After pausing to look at the notice board, which has details of the opening hours and so on on it, she walks to the desk. I decide she could be the address book woman and so I'm expecting her to ask for the book, which I've got in the envelope next to me.

Hello, I say. Can I help you?

Um, she says. I think I left a box on the train. Last night.

Eleven thirty-two, I think.

It was the eleven thirty-two, she says. To Birmingham. I got off at High Wycombe.

Right, I say. Can you describe the box?

It's wooden, she says. About this big.

She makes a gesture to show the size of the box. It seems to be about the size of a shoebox.

Did it have your name on it? I say. Any markings? Handles?

It's not really that kind of box. It's quite old, she says. About a hundred years old. It's got a dark circle on the top.

Sort of a decoration, I say.

No, she says. The dark circle is where a bolt used to go through the wood. It's made from old beams from a schoolhouse in Alaska.

Right, I say. Dark circle, I say, noting it down.

I tell her that's probably enough to be getting on with, take the rest of her details, and that it'll probably turn up. She smiles.

I hope so, she says. I've had it my whole life.

She thanks me, and walks out the door. I watch her as she waits outside the office, before hailing a cab and driving off. I only ever hail cabs at Christmas, when I've been doing my shopping. I find the number of the address book woman and pick up the phone.

* * *

The box woman comes back the next day. She must have been waiting for us to open, because as soon as I unlock the front doors, she comes in. She's wearing a long black coat and a sort of suit beneath it. I guess she had a day off yesterday, I think. The girl I went out with at college wasn't a patch on her.

Hi, she says, before she even gets to the desk. I came by yesterday, about the box.

I nod my head, smiling. The Alaskan box, I say. She smells incredible, I think. Fresh. New.

Yeah, she replies. Did anyone hand it in?

I shake my head. I'm sorry, I say. Not yet. But try again tomorrow.

I'll come back this afternoon, she says. Just in case.

It'll turn up, I say.

You said that yesterday, she smiles sadly. She's really pretty when she smiles.

Yeah, I admit. I say that a lot. But it's true.

She nods, and turns to go.

It must be pretty special, your box, I say quickly. Is there anything inside it?

No, she replies, turning back. It's empty. I was getting the lock on it fixed in London. I usually keep letters in it, airplane ticket stubs, theatre tickets, diaries, that kind of thing.

You must have a bit of a mess on your hands without it, I say. I instantly regret it.

Uh, yeah, she says, after a brief pause. I guess I'll see you later, she says.

Don't worry, I say.

She says, It'll turn up, right?

Yeah.

She waves as she walks out.

I wave back as the door closes but she doesn't see. I don't think I've ever seen Sal wearing a suit. I almost pick up the phone to ask her if she's ever worn one, but decide against it. I'm sure she must have.

Sal made me cheese and ham sandwiches for lunch but I'm not feeling hungry so I go for a walk instead. As I'm walking along New Bond Street I see a suit like the one the box woman was wearing in the window of Donna Karan. It costs a fortune. A young couple come out of the shop, laughing. They're carrying several bags, but not all of them are from Donna Karan. One of them's from Armani.

I look at my reflection in the window. I'm wearing my uniform blue trousers and jumper, with white shirt and grey tie. I look down at my shoes. And back at the suit in the window. I need a new pair of shoes, I think.

We get several dozen items in later that day, the usual assortment of umbrellas, mobiles, rucksacks and coats. And one wooden box, made of reclaimed timber from an old Alaskan schoolhouse.

* * *

She returns just before we close, out of breath. She's carrying her coat under her arm, and in the other holds a black attaché case.

Hello again, I say.

Hi, she says. Did it . . .

Sorry, I tell her. Why don't I give you a call when it comes in?

I'll try again tomorrow, she replies firmly.

Okay, I say. I'll see you then.

I bury my old shoes in the first dustbin I pass, under a copy of the *Daily Express*, and walk home in my new shoes.

* * *

Sal opens the shoebox and takes it out. She looks up at me, smiling.

Shall I open it? she says.

That's what it was made for, I reply.

She turns the key and the new lock opens with a click. With another look at me, she lifts the lid. Then she sits back slightly.

Oh, she says. There's nothing in it.

No, I say, smiling. What do you think?

It's a box, she says.

It's Alaskan, I tell her. Handmade. It's over a hundred years old.

It's, uh, nice, she says.

See that mark there? I say, pointing to the dark circle.

Uh, I think so, she says, peering at the wood.

That's where a bolt used to be, I say. It's made out of wood from an old schoolhouse. In Alaska, I add.

Really? It's lovely, she says. I'm sure we can find something to put in it. It would be good for, uh, needles.

Needles?

Or coupons, she suggests. You know how I'm always losing coupons.

Yeah, I say. You're always losing coupons.

She puts the box on the coffee table and gets up. The

dark, old wood of the box looks strange on the sustainable pine of our IKEA furniture.

Thank you, she says, kissing my forehead. I'm going to make some tea.

As she walks out the room, I pick the box up and open it. In the background I can hear Sal dropping teaspoons into mugs.

I look into the box.

When I open my eyes there's still nothing in it.

HANNAH MCGILL
Dust Is Skin

Hands flat on Rex's desk, throat spasming, I fix my eyes on
the framed dead wife photo that sits by the stapler. She looks
a bit like a cow, the dead wife. She has a big oblong head and
a solid, unwieldy smile. There is an air of immobility about
her. Like you'd need a crowbar to lever her into a vertical
position. Which you would, now. Or is she just bonemeal
and string? How long does it take to rot? Maybe she was
cremated. Maybe she's in here, in a tin can. In an ashtray,
maybe. Silly dead cow. I'm *crying*.

I never could shake off the dead wife; she clung like
dandruff. Imagine if you spilled your ashtray full of human
ashes and they caught in your hair and your eyes and your
clothes – that's how she was for me. A thin coating, never
quite gone. I thought about her a lot. When Rex went
out and left me in the flat – fool – I would methodi-
cally and miserably search his desk and the box files under
his bed, looking for things that would upset me. When I
found tender mementoes – photos of them gawping happily in dated sweaters, love letters, holiday souvenirs – I
would cry and curse. And then I would fold everything
away again and put it back where I found it, wiping my

nose on my sleeve, feeling sadder and less trustful than before.

Ashes. It sounds shocking, doesn't it? The idea of being covered in human remains. But we are, aren't we? All the time. Dust is skin. Dust is skin and hair. *Imperial Caesar, dead and turned to clay.* Think it through and it's no more shocking than what you tolerate every single day, every breath.

Imperial Caesar dead and ... well, he was my English lecturer. Rex. It's such a fucking cliché. I was so irritated with myself – my first week at university, I thought, and I already have a crush on an academic. You can hardly get less original, can you? You might as well conduct an affair with your secretary or go by the name of John Smith. How did I take it seriously? I was seventeen. Everything was serious.

Anyway, it's not like it was totally weird. It's not like he was this dribbling geriatric. He didn't smell old – he hadn't gathered that sour musty old person's air around him yet.

I'm past-tensing him, as if he's dead. Then he'd smell. Dead wife must have smelt rank, even before she went. She died of some hideous wasting thing and by the end she looked like Linda Blair mid-movie. All green dribble and blisters. Well, probably. Come on, I don't know – it's not like he's got a commemorative video. People probably do that. There isn't much people don't do, is there? Anyway, he's youthful, really. Grey ... I'd describe him more fully, but I'm having trouble bringing up his face – my mind is heaving like my throat trying to retch it forth but it's caught. I'm only getting chewed scraps – soft jowls here, tasteful thick-rimmed glasses, tasteful thin lips there. Chewed scraps. Things I have chewed on. The arm of his glasses. Thin lips. Slightly pendulous bristled earlobes which had the stomach-loosening texture of raw bacon. Chubby fingers spiced with pipe tobacco . . . has someone ever done something so awful to you that you're not even angry? Because to be angry would place you back in the world?

I feel like a wound in that moment when it's chalk-white, before the blood rushes in and spills and makes sense. Or I feel like a baby just about to howl – tense, suspended, gathering noise. Only the blood and the noise aren't coming. *This is the Hour of Lead.* (It's Emily Dickinson.) *First – Chill – then Stupor – then the letting go—*

Love that dangling dash at the end, falling off – plop – into space. Letting go. Though maybe Emily just got interrupted by some urgent scouring, or by a visit from a fellow Puritan spinster looking for advice on erotically neutral hats. It's not like I have a library of poets filed neatly in my head, ready to be drawn out and dusted down when occasion demands it. I wouldn't be ready with a spot-on Tennyson dog poem to salve your grazed feelings if your beloved Rottweiler died. But Emily got to me. Rex did Emily, in one of our early tutorials. I clearly remember this beautiful intense boy called Ewan – full girlish lips, a dimpled chin, misunderstood eyebrows – reading his Emily presentation in a hushed and humble voice. Christ, but it was good. It made me blush. He knew every stitch in Emily's rich tapestry. He was *right in there.* He'd built a four-poster bed out of sturdy planks of biography and language and religion and geography, and then he'd brought in a team of intellectual flower girls to garland the whole thing with insight and empathy, and then right in front of us he'd laid sweet Emily down. He'd snuffled right into that tight-laced bodice of hers and insinuated an insistent scholarly hand under all her complicated layers of nineteenth-century petticoating. It was *sexy*. I was terrified. I didn't think that way. I couldn't undress a long-dead poet like that. I couldn't run my fingers through meanings and tease out metaphors like Ewan did (and so unassumingly! So apologetically! Like it was *nothing at all*!). Nope, I was a virgin, still shaky around the rhythm of an iambic pentameter and certainly not comfortable with this kind of nonchalant erudition.

(How did I take it all so seriously? I was seventeen. Everything was serious.)

Casting around the room to see if the rest of Ewan's hushed audience was nodding in cronyish assent, or worse, noting down stylish and penetrating ways in which they might challenge his arguments, I saw Rex looking at me. We looked at each other and I thought, Please, sir, I'm in the wrong place. I should've signed up for an HND in Home Economics at the 24-hour instamatic drive-thru university across the way. I am not equipped to deal with this. I cannot share a table with people who laugh knowingly at jokes about Julia Kristeva. Hell's bells, sir, I'm not even sure whether it's Julia or Julie. Or who the fuck she is.

And Rex thought back: don't worry. You're underlearned, but you're extremely receptive. I can tell. You're curious. That's worth a whole brainful of rote learning. Come and see me after class.

I swear: it happened. I *felt* him comfort me.

You'd think I'd have become wary of close contact with authority figures, after my guitar teacher showed me his collection of autopsy pictures. It's true. His name was Graham and he was a tall man with sallow, pockmarked skin. That makes him sound horribly unattractive, but he wasn't; he had an affecting gentleness and very kind blue eyes. He was shy and polite and he had long, slender fingers. I liked watching him play guitar. I was awful. I got pearly blisters that hurt so much I couldn't practise, which meant my fingers stayed soft and blisterable, and my playing stayed dreadful. Graham liked to play the songs of American female singer-songwriters, the kind who wear ethnic hats and dedicate albums to their cats. Anyway, once I was at Graham's – I must have been twelve – and he abruptly stopped playing whatever masochistic cat-poem he was into at the time. He got up (thin rangy legs, I remember, in pale soft-washed cords) and went over to the bookcase by the window. There he sought out a pile of magazines, which he brought back to the facing wicker chairs in which we held our lessons and handed to me. They were all issues of something called *The Coroner's Report*, cheaply but brightly printed on fuzzy newsprint. The covers showed bodies on tables cut into pieces – flaps of skin pulled back, organs exposed, parts removed and neatly lined up in rows. There were lurid coverlines – 'Decapitation Day', 'Grim Freezer Find', 'Raped And Dismembered'.

I gave them back to him. I was still holding my guitar in front of me. It was a very cheap one, a light thing made of plywood, which had nonetheless earned me the derision of my friends at school, who called me spoilt when I told them that my parents had bought it for me.

'No, look inside,' said Graham, in a voice that I remember as slightly strained.

I shook my head and thrust the magazines at him again.

'You ever seen anything like that before?' asked Graham.

That, you understand, is why I am not a guitar maestro today. I kind of lost the urge. I never told my parents. They thought I just lacked commitment. They shook their heads and looked knowing and weary.

I've just been standing here and there's snot and tears on Rex's fine oak desktop. He keeps a clean house. He hates me to smoke here. Fuck him. I couldn't quell these shakes even if I lit three fags at once – but it's a small oasis of logic at least, a little victory for cause and effect. Why do people smoke? Not because they think it'll make them look like Lauren Bacall, and not because they want to hasten their own demise – but because it makes perfect sense. Each cigarette is a very short story endowed with a beginning, a middle and an end. It always obeys its own rules, and it never goes in for shocking dénouements or unexpected twists. A fag is a fag is a fag – you take it out of its snug little packet, you grip it in your mouth as lightly and effortlessly and intimately as you grip a lover between your legs just after he's come, you breathe in, it hits the back of your throat, you blow out smoke, the fag burns down. You stub it out. No nasty surprises (not until the X-ray you get for your forty-fifth birthday, that is). Always the same – give or take the one in a hundred that tastes a bit sweet and strange like someone's laced it with Nurofen. That's why people smoke in times of crisis or panic. It's not nicotine dependency so much as a desperate scrabble for familiarity. The smoker is not a daring hedonist nibbling on the inner thighs of the Grim Reaper. The smoker is a tedious little coward who wants a regular fix of comforting, straightforward predictability. Might as well have kept right on breastfeeding.

Ash on the carpet. Spilled remains. Well, he won't like *that*.

The laptop computer is sitting in front of me, lid snapped shut, corners fashionably rounded off, like those of a sucked cough sweet. A green light pulses gently at its far rim. It hums to itself. It's as busy and malicious and still as a camouflaged reptile, squatting on the fine dark wood and plotting when to pounce. I could open its jaws again. I let the fag butt slip between my fingers and drop, with a whisper, on to the carpet. It's near my foot but I resist the impulse to stamp out its burning ember. I could open the lid again. As I'm thinking that Rex's key rattles suddenly in the lock. I remember what he said: I might be early today. My four o'clock might not be on. Stay here, why don't you? Use any books you want. But do take care.

Do take care.

I'm still facing the desk and as he's advancing – fussing, hanging his keys on their little hook, picking the second post up from the mat, removing his coat and probably checking the sheen on his bald patch in the hallway mirror with the horrid art deco stained glass panels – I'm thinking about the strangest things. Like: I'll have to give back all his stuff. Not stuff he's given me, but stuff I've taken. I have this awful habit of taking things from people I like. I used to do it with my parents; just absently filch small items of clothing, gloves, sunglasses, scarves – sometimes to wear them and sometimes just to hoard them in my room. It's like kleptomania, except I don't want to keep the things. I want to borrow them. I want to borrow them without asking. I used to do it at school. I remember a teacher – lovely Miss Cates with her high-swept frosted hair – flushed with exasperation, demanding 'What's borrowing without asking? Stealing! Stealing!' And I tried vainly to explain (well-behaved child; clever, too; just this one strange vice . . .) that whilst stealing meant keeping, borrowing meant using and giving back. I wanted the intimacy of a *borrowing* relationship. The freedom to lift things and be trusted to return them.

In later life, I took books and videos and jumpers and corkscrews and fountain pens and calculators and combs from flatmates and lovers and friends. I know, it's clear as day: I wanted insurance against losing them, right? I wanted them to have a reason to come back to me. That's what it's all about, isn't it? Somewhere in the deep, dark, daddy-killing, mummy-fucking recesses of our unconscious minds, we all believe that we can prevent our loved ones skipping the country in dead of night just as long as we retain our grip on their cashmere gloves and their clock radios and their novels by Julian Barnes.

That's why you have to have that dread little ritual in the closing act of any intimate affair: the exchange of plastic bags. The return of random belongings left casually, confidently, arrogantly in the lover's care. The most comprehensive inventories are taken when the break-up is a bitter one, because bitterness and pedantry are bosom chums.

You want no more of me? Then watch me purge you utterly. Have back your gloves, and may you leave them on a barstool at the first singles night you attend. Have back your clock radio, which I have reset so that both you and whoever you wake up with will be a full day late for work. Have back your novels by Julian Barnes, from which I have razored alternate pages and which are no longer fashionable anyway. But wait: there's more. Have back the faded passport photograph of you before I met you, when you still wore glasses and your teeth seemed bigger somehow. Have back the shampoo you left on my shelf in joyous recognition of the fact that we had become intimate enough to accept one another's greasy/oily/problem hair. Have back the small jar of Marmite I kept in the cupboard because you liked it. I have left no stone unturned, no possible hurt uninflicted.

'Oh, you're here?'

He's happy to see me, but there's caution – I haven't spun around to meet him. I'm striving for control. My throat is still heaving, and aches from the effort of holding back sobs. My lower jaw quivers violently and my heart is thudding sick and fast. My face is wet and rubbed raw, salt-stung. *This is the Hour of Lead*, I think. *First Chill. Then Stupor. Then* . . .

'Are you all right?'

I don't turn to face him but I start trying to speak. There's just a raw croak first and then a kind of wheeze and then I say, 'You said I could use your computer.'

Rex is close behind me now and I wonder, will I vomit if he touches me? I can smell him: spicy pipe tobacco, tasteful mature man's cologne, leather and rain and wool. 'What's wrong? What is it? Did you break it? It's –

What was he going to say? It's all right? It's insured? I shake him off me, scuttle across the room, still not looking his way. A rope of mucus dangles from my nose and I drag my sleeve hard across my sore face. Does he know yet what this is about?

'You left some files open, Rex.'

My sobs come like razorblades, each breath between a cacophonous, asthmatic howl. I had thought that he might tell me he had been researching an article. First I thought, still hopeful, that that could be the truth; and then some part of my mind that was still working for him decided that he could employ that excuse, if he thought of it in time, to defend himself. He doesn't, though. Finally – with a gargantuan physical effort – I look at him and see him gazing fixedly at the laptop on the desk. Retracing his steps. *And then I wiped myself off with a tissue from that box and then I went to pack a pipe and pour a whisky and hell's bells it never even crossed my mind to close up my favourite downloads from* Hot Little Under-Tens Learn How to Fuck.

He goes over to the sideboard and pours a whisky, takes it to his big armchair and sits down heavily.

'I was going to talk to you about this.'

'About the fact that I'm a little too old for your tastes? About . . . little . . . children? And *you*?'

'It's something I . . . believe in.'

I can't even prompt him here; I'm gaping like a skull.

'We've talked before about childhood sexuality, haven't we?' he says in his tutor's voice.

It's true; we have. As I recall, we were discussing *Lolita*, and we agreed that a vital step in defending children from abuse was acknowledging their sexual nature and their sexual curiosity (curiosity – worth a whole brainful of rote learning, remember?). We agreed that innocence and purity were dangerous and false notions, and that frankness and openness in matters sexual were crucial. I remember feeling that dizzy little erotic charge you get when you agree quite perfectly with someone you are tentatively coming to love. As your discussion progresses, your voices gather in force and rise in pitch – but *harmoniously*. As *one*. With lots of 'Yes – yes – yes!' and many an 'Exactly!'

He goes on, his voice warm and slow and generous as if he is explaining a simple sum to an imbecile. 'I firmly believe that it is right and beneficial to society as a whole and to children themselves if they are gently and generously guided into the pleasures of sex by a caring adult. It frees them from guilt and it teaches them confidence and trust. It gives them the freedom of knowledge, and that *protects* them from harm.'

This, I ponder, sounds rehearsed. This is rehearsed. For God knows how many years he's waited to be found out. He's got his script down pat.

'It happens that young people are to my taste. That doesn't mean I don't love you.'

I make a jagged noise and spit a mouthful of sour bile right onto his carpet. He looks but doesn't react. He talks on.

'We're not talking about abuse. We're talking about . . . education. Gentle, consensual, pleasurable, non-exploitative—'

I interrupt. My voice is louder than I knew it could be.

'HOT . . . LITTLE . . . UNDER . . . TENS . . . LEARN . . . HOW . . . TO . . . FUCK?'

When he half-smiles I think that I might kill him. I start looking around the room for heavy things. Thing is, I think I borrowed his marble paperweight and took it home in the pocket of my coat. It was cold and nice to touch.

'Listen,' he says intensely. 'Morality doesn't come in neatly packaged absolutes. It changes; it develops. In some societies what I'm saying would be seen as perfectly logical; indeed, necessary for the healthy development of young adults. In some societies, the thought of women working or homosexuals kissing would elicit the same kind of disgust you're feeling now. Sin doesn't exist, and someone as intelligent as you should know that. Look what we've done with the seven deadly sins – we've made them lifestyle choices, haven't we? Don't we celebrate pride as a virtue now? Black pride. Gay pride. Don't we encourage avarice and indulge gluttony and see lust as part of any successful relationship? These things are social, they're societal, they're temporal, they're subject to revision. Tell me: isn't this society fucked up about sex? Don't we all grow up guilty, secretive, lost, embarrassed by our own bodies?'

'Stop lecturing, Rex, for fuck's sake. We're talking about you—'

My voice is constricted and wet, so I hawk onto the carpet again.

'We're talking about you jacking off to a picture of an eight-year-old boy getting—'

'Oh, what will you tolerate, and what won't you?' Rex snaps

suddenly, his pedagogic tone all gone. 'Look, news flash: he liked it. There are kids being beaten and tortured and killed by their own parents, there are kids dying from poverty, there are kids dropping out of school and living by crime. And that's just the children. What's happening to them is happening tenfold to adults. You walk past these people on the street every day. You don't spit or scream or swear. Nine times out of ten you pretend not to hear when someone asks you for spare change. You go home to your comforts and you don't give it another fucking thought because it's just part and parcel of the way the world is. What really horrifies you? Me having a wank.'

Think it through and it's no more shocking than what you tolerate every single day, every breath. Dust is skin and hair . . .

I'm looking at my own scummy saliva glistening on the carpet.

'NO, Rex. You don't get to be a good guy. You don't get to be a good guy. You know this is wrong.'

'I don't accept that it's wrong.'

'Then you won't mind when I tell the university and the police.'

I feel defeated, though, even as I speak. Rex has had years to perfect a martyr's philosophy. And Christ – I'm crying again – by shouting at him, telling on him, ruining his life, will I change what turns him on? Even if I did, it would still turn someone else on. Even if it didn't, there would still be children – what was his melodramatic little phrase? – 'dropping out of school and living by crime'. I would still pretend not to hear when someone asked me for change, nine times out of ten. I am dizzy and exhausted for want of hope. I get up, and my body floods with pain; my muscles have stiffened and cramped up with tension. I walk towards the door.

To my back, my lover says, 'I'll pay you not to.'

JAN NATANSON
Burning

It's happenin.

At last.

It's happenin the day.

Daylicht. Efter aw this time, I'd fair forgot the sky wis sae big. Aw roon there's sic a steir o' stoor an reek, I cannae richtly see. As if the nicht is champin at the bit an willnae bide its time. Or as though awthin I look at is clartit wi soot awreddy.

Mebbe it's ma ain een near blind efter aw that lang time in the dark. They widnae gie us a candle. No even when I begged.

Or mebbe it's ma ain rage roilin roon like a thunnerclood in ma heid an tintin awthin I set ma een on. Sic a storm o' vengefu thochts fae ma coorse black hert. Black as the Earl o' Hell's waistcoat. Aye the very ane they believe is ma true maister – me his servant wummin.

'Whit guid did it dae us, then?' I speired. 'Fell grippy maister shairly, if I didnae even get a new sark oot o' the bargain?'

That was when they first came. When I thocht it wis just

a load o' havers an I could mak them lauch an they would leave us alane.

Afore aw this, I could aye mak fowk lauch. Especially efter a skinfu o' ale. Oh aye, then ma tongue taen aff like a laverock intae a Lammas sky. An ma words could tickle roon fowk's herts an crack even the frostiest face.

Black as the wing on a hoodie craw. A corbie. That's what the Reverend Robertson minded me on as he puffed oot his chest an climbed the stairs to the pulpit. Always that creak, creak, creak at every step. Wis it the auld wood o' the weel worn stairs that gave oot sic a groanin? Or wis it his ain spindly shanks? Or mebbe the ghosts o' lang deid sinners shiftin their doups on the repentance stools?

Aye . . . a hoodie craw, he was . . . wi his black robes an long pointed nose. Lookin doon fae his nest in the pulpit. Jabbing at the congregation like a savage beak at a line o' worms. Devourin aw their kindness – aw their guidness. Leaving them empty. Just shells o' fowk, wi cauld empty crannies whaur their herts had been. Naw, it was even waur than that, for they werenae left empty. The Reverend stappit them fu o' words. Orra hatefu words he found inside the muckle great black book like a deid craw that he cried God's Holy Bible . . .

I can hear his voice dirlin, yet, in ma lugs:

'A good name smells sweeter than the finest ointment.'

Think on these words fae God's Holy Bible. Ye may no be on the repentance stools but that disnae mean that ye are free fae sin. For in the words o' Ecclesiastes – 'There is an evil under the sun which I have seen and it weighs heavy upon men.' Let me tell you there is evil in this toon an I hae seen it.

Aye every mornin ye maun hae seen evil aw richt. Every time ye looked in yer ane keekin gless.

I hae seen evidence o' the maist shameless indulgence in pleisures o' the flesh. Even upricht men wha should ken better hae shown theirsels weak in the face o' the wantonness o' certain loose women!

Mind. It wis Eve brocht sin intae the world; wha listened to the serpent; wha disobeyed God; wha tempted Adam. Wha brocht him doon! Truly a wumman is an unclean sinfu creature by her verra naitur.

You were the serpent – creepin roon wi yer sleekit een an dark sleekit thochts.

In the words of Nahum, 'I am against you saith the Lord of Hosts. I will uncover your breasts for your disgrace. I will count you obscene and treat you like excrement.'

Ye daen that tae aw richt! Monster!

Ezekiel 16 verse 44: 'Did you not commit these obscenities as well as other abominations. And people will say of you "Like mother like daughter."

Ye are a wanton sinner. On Judgement Day will you stand wi the righteous? No. Ye will be cast intae the fiery pit! D'ye ken what it means to burn in everlasting fire? To writhe in agony?

Wi nae hope o' ever findin peace?

Second Chronicles: 'He who practised sorcery and dealt with ghosts and spirits – He did provoke the wrath of the Lord!'

There are evil spirits abroad. I feel the presence of the deil in this place. We must root out those wha dance the deil's reel. For such practices are an abomination and must be stamped out with a harshness that shows no mercy.

If only I could hae put you in the branks like you daen tae me. Aye, a daud o' iron tae stap your mooth. You cheenged fowk intae orra beasts wi yer sermons. It's you wha played the tune an cried oan fowk tae dance. An it wis an ugsome reel roon an aroon the bonfires o' the toon . . .

Exodus chapter 22: 'Thou shalt not suffer a witch to live.'

Thou shalt not suffer a witch to live.

Thou shalt suffer a witch to die though.

And mak her suffer afore her daith.

I can still taste the foostie metal o' the branks in ma mooth, mixed up wi the iron taste o' ma ain bluid whaur they shoved the bridle doon on tap o' ma tongue makin me gag an choke.

I mind on the panic risin up in ma breest then. For I still thocht – if I could only speak tae them – to explain that it wis aw a mistak; that it was the Reverend makin up sic orra lies. If I could just tell them the truth – then they'd hae to believe me. Did they no ken me efter aw?

I seen James MacDonald amongst the guard. An his faither

wis aye sic a guid friend o' ma ain. So he couldnae, shairly? Nane o' them could? They couldnae. They wouldnae? No if they would only listen to me.

But wi that daud o' cauld iron in ma mooth aw hope wis taen awa. They put a bridle on us and syne they treated me like a beast. Waur than a beast. For I kent for a fact that James wis gey saft-hertit wi his ain dugs an sheep an kine.

A haund has shiftit the hood a bittie on ma heid. Despite the reek an stoor, I can see faces. But they're aw tipsalteerie – a mixter maxter o nebs an een an mooths.

An sic a din. Ma lugs are dirlin wi it. But there's tawse roond ma haunds. An it's pulled sae ticht I cannae lift them to stap ma lugs agin that affa roarin din. It soonds mair like cries o beasts than voices o' fowk.

Syne, there's anither noise, droonin oot the rest. A drum? But fae whaur?

Then I realise it's ma ain hert thuddin awa in ma chest. An wi that soond o' fear in ma lugs, I mind back to the darkest time.

Kincaid the pricker wis brocht aw the way fae Fife.

I mind him layin oot his tools. Sae prood o' them. He polished and sherpened and rubbed at them. Picking them up an settin them doon gin they wis playthings an he wis a bairnie that couldnae mak up his mind which ane to play wi first.

They'd taen aff the bridle. I didnae richtly ken for why. Mebbe they wis deaf to onythin I could say to them noo, I thocht. No that I didnae try – wheedlin an sabbin and cryin oot. It had been sae lang since I'd spoke, it soonded strange – a voice I didnae ken I had; sayin words I'm shair I didnae ken afore.

Then ma screams. I thocht they must put the branks back in ma mooth then – if only to save their ain lugs. Sic screams would surely drive them gyte. But syne I saw the truth.

Kincaid wasnae alane.

I saw the minister skulkin ahent him. An although to Kincaid I wis just some kind of orra meat for his skewer, I saw that the minister wis swallowin doon ma hale body wi his een. Slaverin ower ma agony. An wi each scream at cam oot ma mooth his pintle stirred in his breeks an grew big.

Oh then, I wished for the branks back on. I wished that I could hae bitten aff ma ain tongue afore I gien him sic pleisure.

I smell the reek fell strang noo. It's makin me choke. An I hear the soond o crackin wood as the sticks catch and the flames tak ower. I feel the hetness noo. As if aw the hate an anger in the world is turned intae heat. I struggle agin the tawse.

Help me.

I cannae thole the pain.

I cannae thole it.

I cannae . . .

An ma body is suddenly racked wi sabs. Thoosans o sabs – aw jinin intae ae great souch o wund. A fierce wund raivelin up sic a storm. It coorses richt throu me – birlin an dirlin an hurlin – gettin strang-er and strang-er an strang-er.

Then, like a wild beast clawin to get oot – tearin fae ma thrapple comes this great muckle skreich!

And it's me.

In that scream that gaes on and on and on and on. Aw ma pain. Aw ma anger. Aw ma hate – turned intae soond . . .

That skreich – the maist eldrich soond ivver heard.

I see their faces richtly, then.

Aw the toonsfowk . . . Maisie Bell an auld Tammas an Erchie the Hump an James MacDonald . . .

Aw gawpin wi fear at whit they've daen. Their fists held ticht ower their lugs agin that great beast o' a skreich.

At first, I think, they're mebbe richt eneuch – an it is the deil that's cam skreichin up fae deep doon in ma hert.

But syne I ken. Whit cams screamin oot ma mooth is but ma ain daith.

I dinnae need tae thole nae mair.

For tis aw ower.

An then efter aw thon time in the dark, I cam intae the licht.

The sky's sae big.

I'd forgot the daylicht wis sae bricht.

An I can mind oan aw the bonnie things. For there were some bonnie times afore aw this gyteness.

Daunderin doon by the riggs o' a gloamin. The smell o' flooers – sae sweet – t'wid be likes tae turn yer hert as saft as hinnie. An sometimes I'd be daunderin wi a bonnie chiel whase words would be just as sweet an fairly melt ma hert. An syne we'd be aff into the lang gress unner the trees . . .

We'd coorie up in each ither's airms. Aw roon the hinnie-waff o' summer flooers. His daft wurds ticklin ma lugs. His haunds rough wi ferm work but, oh, sae canny as they brocht a warmth to ma body.

Syne we'd lie doon thegither. The grund ablow us. The mune abune. An in atween juist twa bodies rubbin agin each other. That warm feelin floodin richt through me. Twa bodies turnin into flame . . .

I wis aye fond o the nicht sky. I likit to coont the sternies an gaze up at the mune. I likit a daunder doon by the loch side bi the licht o' the mune. The watter gliskin. The birk trees sheenin gin they were made o' siller.

I mind aince, efter ma lad had upped an dressed an gaen away hame tae his femily, just lyin there, by massel. Just watchin the mune an the siller watter an siller trees. Then, I mind, I stood up. But instead o' puttin ma kirtle back on, I took aff aw ma claes. I wantit to feel the saft saft air; to see ma ain body glisk in the munelicht, gin it was made o' siller tae.

A real daft notion cam ower me. To daunce aroon unner that bonnie bricht mune.

To daunce roon an roon. As if the birk trees were a crowd o' fowk at a handfastin party. An I wis the bride. The mune up abune wis ma ain bonnie bridegroom. I daunced an daunced gin ma taes had a life o' their ain. Ma bridegroom mune seemed to be pullin me roon an roon an roon in a reel til ma heid was birlin.

T'wis like I wis fu. Or a gowk.

I felt like I wis fleein throu the air. A laverock soarin on a mune beam. Up an up an up into the air.

Ma hert wis fair loupin wi joy.

Little did I ken that nicht, that amang the black shadows o' the trees wis a hoodie craw. An he wis watchin awthin.

Later it wis, I fund oot he'd been there that nicht. Doon by the watter's edge.

Spyin on us.

Spyin on me.

For though they stappit ma mooth wi a bridle o' iron, they didnae stap ma lugs.

An in that blackness I heard it.

Efter Kincaid went awa.

The creak o spindly shanks as they bent doon to kneel on the flair o' ma cell.

An that voice, I kent sae weel.

No rantin an roarin loud like afore. But low, saft and wheedlin in prayer, moanin like a body in torment.

Oh Lord, save me fae the demon that torments ma ivery thocht. Even in this dark dark place. Even wi ma een shut ticht in prayer I see her yet.

Lilith.

Salome.

Dauncin in the munelicht. Her derk een sheenin. Her bonnie hair pourin ower her shoulders like a rivulet o watter. Her hurdies turned to siller by the mune. Her breests o' alabaster!

Oh Lord, I feel ma verra soul in danger fae sic thochts; fae sic visions sent fae the deil hissel. Help me to be strang. To see her for the demon she is.

Please. I beg You to wipe oot these pictures lodged forever in ma heid.

Jesus, keep me safe. Gie me peace fae sic tormentin thochts.

Jesus Christ Almighty!

Though I feel the verra flames o' Hell lick roon ma soul — Oh God — but I burn for her yet.

I burn for her always.

I burn.

I burn.

JOHN SAMSON
Dry Cleaning

Lachie may not have been descended from the witches of
Broadford, but he foretold that the peat-cutting robot would
fail. It lasted fifteen minutes before being defeated by midges.
DJ had brought it back from the Highland Show along with
an electronic byre deodoriser. This was borrowed, never to be
returned, by the postmistress. She has no byre.

One year on and Lachie, elder son of Hettie and Donald,
who fled crofting for the good life as estate agents in Bearsden,
sits glowering behind the *Oban Times*. A packing case is
being scraped across the lino. He focuses desperately on
reports from the WRIs: votes of thanks, calendar-making
competition results. But all of this cannot obliterate the
fraternal greeting. 'You'll have to see it sometime. It's a
Dipless Sheep Dip.'

There is something cold and ungracious about tightly rolled
newsprint invading a nostril, a trick Lachie picked up watching
the Pamplona Bull Run on Grampian. But DJ was not to
be deterred. Within the hour DJ the clever one, MacBrain
himself, had assembled what Lachie took to be poles of a
fancy tourist tent. They glowed even in the light of a summer
evening. Glowed like the hands on old Captain Jamieson's

watch when he would put it in his trouser pocket and exhort the children to peer in.

'The rays do the business for the sheep but there's no nasty side-effects like with organophosphorus. The lassie who explained it to me said it was dead easy to work, kept repeating "ewes are friendly". Cheeky besom I never took her on.'

Mollified by a half-bottle, Lachie stroked his thinning hair and stared at the apparatus. 'If it works OK maybe we could hire it out to the rest of the Clach. Yes . . . "Let us cleanse your flock for a small sum. Come to the Wee Fee Presbyterians—"

'Anyway better switch it off before its batteries go.'

'Actually it has none, nor mains either. It runs on these isotope things which never really run out. So, um, she said.'

Looking back, Lachie wondered why he kept so calm. Maybe he had seen in DJ something of Jack bringing home the magic beans.

Next day on a gentle brae worthy of a dance routine by Gene Kelly (if he had had a good eye for bog and droppings) the brothers set up the Dipless Sheep Dip. Tosh the collie stared at the luminescent rods and decided against raising his leg. In the Clach, no news spread faster than death or failure. So the prospect of the latter had drawn a group of locals imbued with whatever is the Gaelic for *Schadenfreude*.

Tosh relished this audience and hammed it up, imagining he was on *One Dog and His Man* (as he preferred to call it). DJ reckoned the sheep should go through the frame at the same speed as for a wet dip so he scattered a few bits of turnip to delay their progress. Old Captain Jamieson, having just arrived, thought the contraption was for some kind of satanic ritual. This made him think of social workers, which made him nervous.

Young Cal was first to inspect the outcome of this dipless dipping. He felt qualified to do so having left for Glasgow University Vet School last October, only to return in the December. But he still wore the check shirt with the tiresome tie bearing an up-to-the-elbow-in-cow motif. Cal declared the sheep free from live parasites and seemed very impressed. Others concurred, disappointed by the lack of failure but now intrigued with the result. Sensing this mood change, Lachie nudged DJ. Within ten minutes some kind of hiring arrangement had been made.

During the days that followed DJ at last found a use for the large zip pocket at the rear of his catalogue wax jacket, made in Spain by Barbour of Seville. It was just the place to keep cash paid by locals enterprising enough to lease the Dipless Sheep Dip. He was counting the week's takings when Lachie delivered another nudge. Years of interpreting Lachie's nudges meant that he did not have to look up from the bundle of grubby notes to know that bother approached.

Old Cal, stocky and red-faced was making purposeful, if irregular, strides in their direction. He had Roddy the ram on a tether and the beast was not keen on covering the ground. Nor was it keen to cover ewes, a situation Cal Senior bluntly blamed on the glowing rods. He demanded recompense. Wanted Roddy to be replaced. And not by DJ thank you very much. He had heard that joke on the Scottish Home Service.

The brothers paid for the vet – thin ginger moustache, expensive anorak, stupid boots – to take samples of Roddy's vital fluids. Three days later the ram was pronounced sound. This news infuriated Cal but neither did it put DJ and Lachie at ease. It was time again to commune with the Talisker. An awful hypothesis dawned upon DJ and he needed the postmistress to test it.

Her unrequited lust for Lachie was legendary. Having set up the glowing tubes around the crofthouse door, DJ sent for the postmistress on the pretext of helping Lachie with his passport application. This heady mix of sex and travel proved irresistible. She bustled in, wearing a figure-hugging Pacamac, and stared onion-eyed at Lachie who was sitting in the foetal position clutching, for protection, a virgin copy of *Life and Work*. 'See you Lachie you big hairy boy I could have the trousers off you and . . . and . . . give them a damn good press.' With that she was gone.

In the silence which followed Lachie and DJ exchanged Significant Nudges. The gross of Curly Wurlies, left over from The Millennium was retrieved from the scullery and scattered on the floor. DJ telephoned an urgent grocery order to the Store by the Shore and awaited Chunky Dunky, the delivery boy possessed of a biblical gluttony. Young Duncan duly arrived and carried the box through to the table, treading upon his favourite confectionery. He looked down with unprecedented disinterest, accepted a tip and left. Silence returned. The half-bottle conference resumed.

DJ, who sometimes listened to Radio 4, had heard about genes. Scientists could make up a person just by following a sort of knitting pattern. A glimmer of insight brought DJ slowly to his feet. 'Maybe this Dipless Dip has been interfering with these gene things.'

But Lachie it was who made the ultimate conceptual leap: 'Ginger face would have noticed something odd in the samples. No, this contraption of yours cleanses right enough. Washes away Sin; so far Lust and Gluttony.'

The brothers purchased whisky only in half-bottles because the shape lent itself to rapid concealment during surprise ministerial visits. Empties stack intimately enough to minimise tell-tale clinking during disposal. And two halves are more accurately divisible by two. Several were emptied as they considered if Roddy the ram could have original sin. Had the delivery boy also lost excessive interest in certain sections of his mother's catalogue? Was the process at all selective? Had they themselves been cleansed? Clearly not. Avarice was certainly still present.

'Never mind hiring out for the dipping. This could earn us a fortune in the dieting market,' said DJ. 'Look what it did for Chunk's appetite. No Gluttony, see? There's a couple of fat Yanks at the B and B just now, fair eating Mrs Morrison out of lamb chops. I'll go and make a diplomatic approach. These Americans are forever looking for easy ways to slim.'

The MacDonalds of Rochester NY had come to the Clach in search of the cottage from whence their ancestor had been cleared; cleared to make way for the sheep whose descendants they now ate, literally, with a vengeance. DJ came to call upon the exotic couple and Mrs M generously waived the viewing fee. Mr and Mrs MacDonald introduced themselves as Marion and Steve respectively and confusingly.

DJ's pitch was that he was a humble entrepreneur, much like their forebear and would they be interested in a lifestyle product which could improve self-esteem without surgery, diet or exercise? Steve smiled slowly and twinkled through her flicked-up spectacles. Marion turned purple to the crown of his pate. 'My wife got off that stuff at the Betty Ford you . . .' The expletive jolted DJ into a direct approach. 'I've got something that can drastically cut down your intake of food. You'll lose all that weight with no effort at all.' He decided against finishing the sentence with a reprise on the 'at all' lest NBC had screened Para Handy and he was mistaken for the devious skipper.

Marion seemed relieved that the subject was body shrinking rather than mind expansion. DJ described his equipment and its effect on Duncan. They knew him as a sort of room service waiter who made thrice daily trips to the B and B delivering top-up rations to complement Mrs Morrison's already generous meals. Sometimes he had accepted tips in the form of Gypsy Creams and they were impressed by his ability to finish a packet between the door and his bicycle.

They agreed to a trial.

Next day the American couple visited the croft. By now the brothers had carefully avoided catching any of the rays from the tubes, wrapping them in pages torn from *Scottish Farmer* until needed. Had they looked closely at this wrapping they would have seen a product recall notice referring to one faulty Dipless Sheep Dip.

As arranged, Marion and Steve had arrived immediately after finishing Mrs M's cholesterol-laden breakfast twice over. They stayed outside while DJ carefully set up the tubes around the door again and Lachie prepared a platter of sizzling lamb chops. The wife was to be subjected to the rays. For comparison, her equally overeating husband would not.

'Ready Steve,' said DJ. 'Walk fairly slowly through the glow.' Redundant advice, since her wide beam ensured such a tight passage that DJ feared for the tubes. Once through, she cast but a glance at the chops before ignoring them completely and studied instead Lachie's long johns drying by the fire. Neither food nor manly undergarments could set her juices flowing.

'How is it, honey?' called her husband. In his eagerness to find out he almost entered before DJ could dismantle the tubes. Once inside he repeated the enquiry between mouthfuls of fast-cooling lamb. His wife replied with an obscure reference to the culinary tradition where sheep are stuffed into pigs, adding 'And you can sleep in your own sty tonight.'

Lachie fractionally beat DJ to the Nudge. What eloquence there was in that elbow-rib sibling contact. Translated it meant Do The Talking And Fast. DJ did his best. 'You see, thanks to this device, Mrs MacDonald will have less weight on her.'

'Indeed,' replied Mr MacDonald. 'The weight being me.'

They had left, threatening litigation if the effects were permanent. The brothers were worried. They began discrete enquiries of the Storekeeper about how many trips Duncan was making to the B and B. After three days the rate seemed to be restored. After ten, Duncan himself was seen gnawing on a caramel bar. At three weeks Lachie felt the old uncomfortable feeling when he went to buy TV licence stamps from the postmistress. It was the way she licked them for Lachie before grinding them into his book But nearly two months passed before DJ witnessed the event which brought relief and inspiration:

Roddy, amidst a haze of midges, attempting congress with a tree stump.

He could not remember running home nor calling for Lachie to set up the half-bottles. Hardly a decent nip later, DJ had explained almost all. 'Body mass. The smaller it is the longer the effect. Get the rods. We're off to our peat bog.'

The brothers laid the rods like some giant matchstick puzzle so that they criss-crossed pools of stagnant water. Then they retreated from the scourge of the West Highlands.

The female midges are the worst. Bloodsuckers, real gluttons. And while Lust is a nebulous concept in the insect world there is always scope for the male to refrain from its equivalent. The glowing bars drew them in their thousands and defused their devilment. The result transformed the Clach.

It won the English Tourist Board's prestigious Only the Prices Sting award. Tourism boomed as word spread that the local midges were friendly. DJ was head-hunted to become Professor of Bio-ethics at Hebridean University. Lachie, left to dose on double half-bottles, consented to marry the postmistress. For a wedding present, DJ gave them the peat-cutting robot. It worked perfectly.

JANET FRANCES SMITH
Fancy Footwork

We fell in love over a simple fungal infection. He walked into
my life almost as quickly as I walked into his consulting rooms.
But he was good at fancy footwork, as I discovered later.

To this day, the smell of surgical spirit makes me feel
quite heady. A lot of passion can throb under a smart white
professional coat.

At the time, my life was on hold. I was wondering which
way to jump. January is a month for reflection and for forward
planning. Chill, crisp winds circle round houses and shopping
centres blowing away last year's discarded aims and desires.
Brown earth becomes glazed with frosts. Clear nights show
silver stars against coal-black. Snowdrops nod. Clouds are sod-
den with the promise of snow. It was time, time to write my
resolutions, a habit ingrained in me like letters in Blackpool
rock, since I was old enough to hold a chewed pencil.

My damp calf-skin crimson boots mouldered by the door
as the gas fire hissed out heat into the dank air of my small
bedsit. Behind a curtain patterned with great orange suns
lay the waste of my last three meals, a takeaway curry still
threatening with its raw odour.

Resolution One. Get a life.

Resolution Two. Buy hair straighteners.

Resolution Three. Wash up daily, or at least weekly.

The list didn't have the snap or crackle of previous years. The missing ingredient was zest.

Friends at work urged me to take up sport. So I bought a pair of trainers and signed up at the local gym. There I learned about the amazing elasticity of Lycra and wondered if I could make my fortune marketing Lycra shopping bags which expanded as you added yet another swede, a pound of carrots, a stone of potatoes . . .

I trod the treadmill, worked with the weights, sweated on the cycle. I stretched and groaned and strained through the remains of January and all of February.

I never knew it was possible for a woman to sweat so much. The glow I was used to became something of a torrent. Rivers ran between my breasts. My hair curled wildly across my forehead. My groins were humid. A ray of sunshine and I was enveloped in rainbows.

My feet didn't escape. That smell of cheese wasn't my singles tea of Welsh rarebit. It was my feet. And very soon the skin between the fourth and fifth toes on both feet began to itch.

By this time it was spring and romance was about to walk into my life. Gaudy crocuses spread carpets of colour on the grassy verges. People looked up and smiled as they passed me by, as if released from winter prisons. Coats were loosened. Scarves sloughed off. Daffodils paused before their yellow rash ran through the grass. Children swarmed in the park, winter-locked energy bursting forth. Kites flew. Dogs barked. Trees budded.

Even gnarled grandfathers were coaxed onto mossgreen wooden benches.

Love was in the air.

I found love in the Yellow Pages and not the lonely hearts section.

R.G. Onions was a Chiropodist with letters after his name and a brass plaque to put them on. Mother always wanted me to marry into medicine. I suspect that was the reason for her hypochondria – the doctor was rarely off our doorstep. She never realised he was as gay a checked tablecloth.

The consultation began with a man at my feet. That was a first. His white coat crackled with starch. He had a noble-shaped head, with perfectly formed ears the colour of discreet ladies' underwear.

Mr Onions, seated attentively on a shiny leathered-covered footstool, spotted the trouble straight away.

'Footwear creates the necessary conditions of moisture and warmth between the toes,' he said cradling my foot in his soft white hands. 'And communal activity permits the spread of infection.'

Infection? I shuddered at the word.

'Have we been wearing trainers?'

I nodded.

'And do we train at the gym?'

I nodded again.

'Hmmm,' he said. 'We've been using communal chang-ing rooms.'

I gazed down at the shiny, balding head. It seemed to glisten in the stark white of the first-floor surgery where Mr Onions had his chiropody practice. Voices echoed in here, bouncing off the sterile emulsioned walls.

Then he looked up at me. His face softened. His eyes behind the thick spectacle lenses were a brilliant blue. They reminded me of gobstoppers behind a bull's eye window in a sweet shop in the York museum.

'A common fungal infection,' he said. 'Athlete's foot.'

'It itches so,' I said.

He stroked my foot. 'At least we've caught it in time,' he said.

I saw him glance sideways at my shoes, placed neatly on the floor beside his consulting couch. The veins in his neck thickened. I'd been wearing the black patent two-and-a-half-inch heels with the ankle strap. Totally unsuitable, which is why I liked them. The ticklish warmth of a spring day had urged me to wear them. I liked the click, click, click that followed me everywhere. Posters on the consulting-room walls showed shoes straight from a dyke's wardrobe, laced-up and sensible. I waited for the lecture. Would it be damage to parquet flooring, damage to a woman's skeletal frame or the more information-bent lecture about the weight on a stiletto being the equivalent to the weight of three mature elephants? None was new to me.

But he said nothing about them. Familiar now with the ways of sweat, I watched tiny glistening pin heads spout from his balding head. They sparkled like miniature diamonds under the harsh light from the neon strip above us.

'Toenails can also become infected,' he remarked, wiping the back of his hand across his forehead. 'The nail becomes thickened, brittle, yellowish-brown in colour, eventually developing a "worm-eaten" or porous appearance.'

His long supple fingers teased cotton wool from a tube. He upturned a glass bottle, wet the end of the cotton wool, and, cradling my other foot, dabbed at the offending areas of skin.

'Tell me,' he said turning those bright blue eyes on me again, 'do you always wear such high heels?'

I shrugged. The glass in his spectacles flashed like a signal. Under his gaze it would be like owning up to doing a line of cocaine every day.

'Now and then,' I lied. Mother had always been free with the word 'tart' when I tottered out of the house. High heels, I felt, made me look like less of a sad single. Mr Onions's breathing had altered. There was a rasping sound in his chest. A spate of coughing cleared it.

'Infections can spread,' he said. 'Do we share a towel – with our husband?'

'I'm not married,' I said.

'I think, Miss Er . . .' he said, gazing up at me through thick spectacle lenses. His pupils had expanded to become dark pits of blue-black.

'Ms Bender,' I said. 'Carol Bender.'

He shuffled on his footstool and returned his gaze to my feet.

'I think, Ms Bender,' he said, 'that we also have a corn. Here?'

I sucked the air in between my teeth as he applied pressure to a spot on my little toe.

'Aaah,' I said.

He looked at me then and I thought of April mornings, broom laden with pale yellow blossom, bees heady with their first taste of spring nectar. He smiled, and although he could have done with a visit to an orthodontist to straighten out what were rather uneven teeth, it was a smile that pierced my gloom.

'Wear flip-flops in the changing rooms, Ms Bender,' he said. 'Choose hosiery made from natural fibres. Use an anti-fungal powder.'

It was as though he was reading from a manual of Podiatric Medicine, but there was such a warm timbre to his voice. It was as soothing and as settling as a first drag on a forbidden cigarette.

'Those high heels,' he said. 'Tut, tut, tut. How fashion conspires to create work for chiropodists.' He followed that with the smile again.

He chose a swan's neck probe, one of the gleaming chrome instruments, from a metal tray. The noise was like looking for a teaspoon in a cutlery drawer. It rang in my head like wedding bells. Head bowed, he began his work. I could see small silver hairs sprouting from his ears, like tiny creatures coming up for air.

'I have two tickets for The Society of Chiropodists and Podiatrists annual ball,' he said. I noticed his hands – now holding my toes as he clipped the nails. They were damp. 'I wonder if . . .'

'I'd love to,' I said.

The evening was a glorious success. I wore a pair of red high-heeled shoes. They had thin wispy ankle straps and my toe nails, painted Rimmel's Hot Red, peeped out prettily. Mr Onions spun me round the dance floor like a swirl of candy floss.

During the last waltz he whispered in my ear.

'High heels distort the skeletal frame and are the root causes of calluses and bunions.'

The damp patch his hand made on the back of my polyester dress never came out.

When Raymond Onions and I were married, we moved into his house, a tall Edwardian terrace with a basement and three floors above.

Things in the bedroom department were passionate, bordering on the bizarre. I wasn't shocked. I might have been a 43-year-old spinster when we married, but I knew that S & M wasn't an alternative department store. My high heels featured in most of what we did. We used a lot of post-coital Elastoplast. And we kept up to date with our tetanus jabs.

Mother would have been appalled that a man with a brass plaque could stoop so low. But then he was a chiropodist. And as a non-conformist, he was unfamiliar with the word sin.

So what went wrong?

Instead of New Year resolutions, he listed my bad habits and posted them on the bulletin board in our kitchen. There was a dent in his thumb where he had pushed the pin. It remained for hours.

The habits were:

1. Leaving used floss on the bedroom floor.
2. Keeping a used handkerchief under the pillow.
3. Wearing knickers a second or third day.

There were ten misdemeanours altogether. Not criticism, Raymond had said, but character-building improvements.

He went away in March to the Birmingham Conference

of the Society of Chiropodists and Podiatrists at the Grand Hotel, Colmore Row. There was the Scientific Programme, the Trade Exhibition and the Social Programme. The latter involved a Caribbean Party where grass skirts were welcome but optional.

I wasn't to go. It would be boring, said Raymond.

While he was away, I planned a thorough spring clean of my new home. The March sun had blazed a trail through the windows, like the beam of a sentry's torch. Dust had to be wiped and sucked away. Clutter needed driving out. I planned to consign it to the attic. The drop-down aluminium ladder was easy to use. A light switch was just by the hatch. I poked my head through. A fluorescent light tube buzzed and crackled as the electric current shot through.

It illuminated row upon row of stiletto-heeled shoes, all colour co-ordinated. Rows of pale pink merged into pretty pink and from there to deep pink. Black and patent were intermingled. Silver and gold were set out separately.

There were about three times as many as the local Dolcis. All with impossibly high heels. I am married to the Imelda Marcos of Ormskirk, I thought as I stepped onto the floorboards.

The shoes were all a size nine-and-a-half. Raymond's size. A trunk revealed a horde of what Mother would have called tart's clothing.

Hot pink featured a lot. There were blonde wigs that were pure Dusty Springfield. And fishnet tights.

And Raymond had told me he shaved his legs to be hygienic.

I rehearsed the conversation I would have when he returned.

Maybe I'd start by asking if he had worn a grass skirt to the Caribbean evening.

But he arrived in a taxi – with another woman.

'This,' he said, 'is Miss Blow. She's a state-registered chiropodist with no job and nowhere to live.'

He wiped his glasses on his cardigan as the warmth from the house steamed up the lenses.

'Carol, meet my new partner.'

Miss Blow walked into our lives in a pair of beige Nubuck flatties, which Raymond said had excellent support for her metatarsal arches. She wore cotton hosiery and did not share a towel. She took the spare bedroom, next to ours, seriously curtailing the ecstasy and agony that can be inflicted during copulation with a pair of stilettos.

I found I couldn't mention the attic.

Meal times became a discussion ground for what they had met in surgery that day. Diabetic feet were discussed over Dover sole. Veruccas over veal. Bunions over bangers and mash. Leg ulcers over leek-and-potato pie.

I took to having a Pot Noodle at four before they came home.

I took up fencing. The cut and thrust, the white clothes, the clash of steel on steel soothed me.

When I got home, they'd often been practising with bandages. Then one day, Miss Blow came home alone. Raymond, she said, was tussling with a particularly nasty ram's horn toe nail and, would I believe it, the woman had a plantar fasciitis on the other foot! He would be tied up for ages.

She laughed at this as though it had, for her, a double meaning.

She had tiny white teeth graded like a pearl necklace. Her skin had the sheen of someone about to blush. Her hair was a shiny bob, with wispy bits trailing down the nape of her neck. Her hands were strong and capable with square nails.

'I'm having a bit of trouble with my left hallux,' I said, having picked up some of the jargon in the months of my marriage.

She unpeeled my support hose and gave my big toe a close inspection. I lay back and thought of England. Soon she was sucking my toe, which I know isn't correct chiropody procedure, having shared bed and board with the chairman of the local branch of the Society of Chiropodists and Podiatrists, motto Post Curam Otium – after healing, leisure.

Miss Blow and I had moved onto something else. Something better.

'Those high heels you wear,' she said, as well as one can with a hallux in one's mouth. 'Wear some for me, now.'

Book of Job

Heaven could be an eternity of God asking, 'What happened?' and Jesus asking, 'Why did I bother?'

Book of Job: 1: Lust

So, what happened?

There's this one club just up from the docks. We call it the Green Triangle because, I don't know, we just do. It's a cool name. Well, it doesn't really have a name because it's not really a club, not legally anyway. It's just a warehouse, actually, where everyone goes. Well, not everyone, y'know, just everyone who goes there.

So, what happened?

Well, I was there with a friend of mine. We'd done a couple of snow cones before we arrived. Snow cones. Well, it's like speed through a water-pipe, y'know? Anyway, so we'd done a couple and we were at this club and I was just sitting down. Y'see behind all the scaffolding near the stairs there's a whole bunch of sofas and I was just there, sitting there and this guy sort of sat down next to me and he said he had some x, ecstasy, and he gave me some so I had some of that too. He seemed . . . I thought he was cool because I've never met anyone who does x who isn't. I thought he was a skater because he dressed kinda like that, all baggy and cute but in retrospect I know he was lying because he was just a fuckwit.

So, what happened?

I went away with him. Away from the club. We just left. I never told my friend. I couldn't find her so we just left. He had a car. It was really big like one of those big old 70's cop cars like a Buick or a Holden or a Chevy or something. Y'know, like from *Starsky and Hutch*. He said he'd borrowed it from a friend in the army who had to stay in the barracks that night. It was grey, like silver-grey, and the interior was plush and really clean and I lit a cigarette cuz my head was fucked and he hollered at me about how rude and impolite it is to smoke in someone else's car, 'the height of rudeness'.

So, what happened?

So I put it out and I guess I must've looked pretty bad – scared or something because he apologised and gave me another pill but I didn't actually know what it was, that one or the first one, I just took it and then we drove for ages and ages and got to an apartment building in some suburb but I don't know which except that it was inner – I think it was inner-west but it might've been by the coast but that's east then we parked and walked for ages up flights of stairs and down corridors and I asked if it was OK to smoke now and he said yes of course it was OK and then we walked into an apartment, number 712, brass numbers on the door and a peephole but I guess all doors have that. The hinges creaked. He had a key on a key-ring. One of those big bunches of keys like a gaol-warden. I tripped over something when we went inside. I just couldn't really see straight anymore. My head was pretty fucked.

So, what happened?

There were other people inside. Men. I'm not sure how many. More than three less than twenty. Just a lot them.

So, what happened?

I can't tell you. I just can't.

Book of Job: 2: Envy

So, what happened?

I was staying at my . . . my boyfriend's apartment that night. I was asleep in his bed and I heard the bedroom door open and woke up. Kept my eyes closed. There were at least two men in the room. I could feel them. I could feel the weight of them standing in the doorway looking at me, at my supposedly slumbering form.

So, what happened?

Well, then I heard them speak.

'Isn't it incredible?' That was my . . . boyfriend. He pulled the covers off my body. 'Man, she sleeps stark naked like that every night.'

'Give you five for a go at her.' One of his friends. I don't know. I don't know who.

'Man it'd cost you five just for the bed. This is my woman we're talking about here.'

'Okay, how about seven?'

'Practically rape. Make it fifteen.'

'Get fucked. She doesn't look that good.'

'Well you wouldn't know unless you tried.'

So, what happened?

Well, then they laughed and walked back out of the room closing the door behind them.

I sat up in bed.

I could get dressed. They'd know I heard them and then I'd be a liar for pretending to be asleep. I could leave. They're just in the next room between me and the front door. Maybe it was just a joke? Maybe it wasn't. I'll just go back to sleep and forget about it. No I won't. He tried to sell me!

Those thoughts were slipping through my mind at lightning speed. Panic bile in my throat. That horrible just before vomit feeling.

Ten minutes, I'll pretend I just woke up and need to take a walk.

So, what happened?

I donned my clothing and perched on the edge of his bed watching the clock. Listening next door. Praying they wouldn't come back in. Then there was a noise from the next room. Men's voices. Then a woman's voice slurring, drunk or drugged. The sound of someone falling over.

So, what happened?

What in the name of God is going on?

Then a scream. I went to the window, climbed out onto the fire escape and left.

Book of Job: 3: Pride

So, what happened?

I don't like that part of town but I had business over there. A meeting that ran a tad late. My line of work gets like that at times. The docks can get quite dangerous at that time of night so I was in a hurry. My bike, it's a Kawasaki ZX12R, was in the parking lot. The lot by the pier twelve. I saw a girl walking towards the same lot. She was with a guy. I don't know what guy, just a guy. I couldn't describe him. I couldn't even see him. It was all shadows. That pixel-painting look that darkness does to vision.

So, what happened?

They seemed pretty wasted but all the kids around there

always do. There's that abandoned repository at the end of the pier that's used for raves or something every weekend. I don't know. I don't go. I was never really into that shit. I like jazz.

So, what happened?

The couple left the warehouse together. I assume they were a couple. They came down the stairs and started across the carpark at about the same time as I did but from the opposite direction. Their car was parked near my bike. It wasn't there when I arrived that afternoon. I know that because if it had've been I wouldn't have parked anywhere near it. People who drive those big old cars are always bad drivers. Without exception. Especially when there's a bike near them. And a bike driven by a woman? No way would I have parked anywhere near that thing. The drivers think they're indestructible. They're in tanks, for fuck's sake, what do they expect? I'm a good driver but there's nothing you can do against a ton of steel bearing down on you. So, when I saw them heading for that car in the state they were in I almost ran.

So, what happened?

She was walking behind him. I guess a few steps behind him. At one point she stumbled and fell against a Hyundai and he grabbed her arm and pulled her up. The same way you'd pull a disobedient dog. I don't know, maybe I'm reading too much into it now. He could've been giving her a helping hand like you help a child or a little old lady or something. I don't know. It seemed like he was dragging her along. But maybe she needed that. Or maybe she just wanted it.

So, what happened?

They reached the car at the same time I got to my bike and I was getting my helmet and my gloves on and my jacket zipped up as they were getting into the car. It looked like she was in a pretty bad way. He had to help her in. She said something to him or did something. What was it?

So, what happened?

Oh that's right. She lit up a cigarette. I could see it through the windscreen. He hollered something at her really loud. I couldn't hear the words but it was loud then he slapped her but the car was already started by that time so I just left.

Book of Job: 4: Sloth

So, what happened?

Once upon a time there was a little girl who lived in a jungle. She fed on fruits and nuts. Every week she'd go to the waterhole to be a part of the community. She would try to fit in; oh they would all try. All the little animals: all the little girls and boys and somehow in their common sense of disparity they found a comforting conformity. But then one week the little girl left and never came back.

So, what happened?

She went to sleep with a coin under her tongue to pay her way across the River Styx. It happens to the best of us, baby. A pyramid of dust, a tablet of gold, a drop of mercury. Whatever. Charon gets his fee. That's the way of it.

So, what happened?

I was on the couch in the Green Triangle. It's my couch. I'm always there. The animals come and the animals go but I always remain. Actually it's a green leather couch, which I think is a nice touch. So, this girl comes over. They always do, eventually. I hear what they say about me. Ugly and fat, fat and ugly. But I have what they want. I always have what they want. They always come and they always come back. She came and she got what she wanted. Then a young lad came along and took her by the hand. Gave her some Rohypnol and told her it was x. It wasn't. I should know. I sold it to him. But it's a dangerous world and she wanted to live in it.

So, what happened?

She left with him, of course. Who am I to blow against the wind?

*   *   *

Book of Job: 5: Anger

So, what happened?

She was my best friend. We did everything together. Everything. Then she pissed off with some guy I didn't even know. Without me. Without **me**. I saw them leave. She was wearing my dress that night. She'd come over to my place and we got ready together. She didn't have anything to wear. She never does, y'know. She always wears my stuff. I picked out a dress for her. It's so cool. I would've worn it but she's my best friend. She was my best friend. So I let her have it. I fuckin' hope he did, too.

Book of Job: 6: Avarice

So, what happened?

I was over at my friend's house with the guys. We were having a few beers watching *The Zone*. It's kinda lame but it's got some cool bands on. So, the guy who owns the place says he wants to show me something. We go into his room and there's his current girlfriend, like, totally naked on his bed. Out like a light. Beautiful. He scored well this time. Problem was he knew it.

So, what happened?

We all share. We're friends, that's what friends are for. So he asked me if I wanted to have a go at her. Well, of course I would've but the price was too high. Yeah, we charge each other for use. Hey, you've gotta make rent somehow. So we hit the sofa again and watched the rest of the show. I was thinking of how I could get a piece of his new girl. It's pretty bad but I was actually thinking of getting her phone number and doggin' her behind his back. I don't like to think I actually thought about that but I've gotta be honest with myself. Hey, I've got nothing against him being mercenary but fifteen bucks? That's theft.

So, what happened?

Well another guy we know came in then. He has a key to the place. I think he lives there.

So, what happened?

Uh, I couldn't really say.

Book of Job: 7: Gluttony

So, what happened?

Oh yeah. She was nice.

So, what happened?

My flatmate has a girl at the moment. She's cute. Very nice girl. I was with her a year or so ago. That's how they met. Isn't that sweet? I think that's sweet. She wasn't really my type, though. I dumped her. Gently of course. I'm very good that way. It's a gift.

I'm in retail. That's my line. Great way to meet chicks, huh? I know that's what you're thinking. And you'd be right if you're into mass-market chicks. I'm not. My girl's gotta have that something special, y'know what I'm saying? She's gotta put out because I've got a need. I know alotta guys use the 'blue ball' line on girls just to get 'em to screw and you know what? I think that's fucked, cuz it gives guys like me a bad name. I really – no I'm serious – if I don't get laid I am in pain. Serious physical pain.

So, what happened?

I started renting a room with this guy about a year and a half ago and man, y'know what? He understands. He really does. He understands that some men have needs. Of course it pays off for him cuz he gets the girls when I'm done. Also he wouldn't have known about the Green Triangle if it weren't for me. I have connections in the retail industry and the Green Triangle is the most awesome place in town. It's set up by a clothing store. Very chic. It's twenty-five bucks in but worth every penny, I feel. It's what the kids want.

So, what happened?

Y'know, personally I'm not into drugs. They're just not my bag. It's too much of a scene thing. I prefer to be an individual. But some people, particularly women, enjoy them as a relaxation device. I understand this. I'm very . . . open-minded.

Did you know that Rohypnol been dubbed 'the rape drug'?

Now, I think that's ridiculous. It's just a relaxant, that's all. It diminishes the inhibitions, allows people to act the way they really want to if society would only accept people for who they are. Some people use it unwisely, I concur, but that's what experimentation is all about.

So, what happened?

I have a supplier. A guy who hangs out at the Tri. Well, he doesn't so much hang out as practically fuckin' live there if you know what I mean. I don't think he could leave even if he wanted to. He's practically welded to the sofa. But he's tolerated because he's discreet. Actually I think he's just too indolent to be indiscreet.

Well, when I saw the young lass he was attempting to chat up I just had to save her. I mean, the guy's a waster. So I slipped her some Rohypnol. I told her it was ecstasy cuz some people feel a little weird, nay, apprehensive. It has such a bad reputation. I must say, it hit her pretty hard. I guess she's pretty new to the scene. I practically had to carry her to my car.

When we finally got to the flat – it was a long and grueling ride. I was starting to have second thoughts. I mean the girl had no manners but I have my balls to consider and, man, they can really drive a guy's life, y'know? And all in all she was mighty fine.

So, what happened?

The boys were pretty happy when they saw what was on offer for the evening. Actually they got a little over-excited. I'm happy to just talk for a while. Get to know each other, kinda thing, before we get down to the business at hand. But the boys had had a few drinks and before you knew it, she was tied to the chair with a telephone cord and they were all having a go. Well, I got in first of course.

Book of Job: 8: Self-Obsession

What happened.

There is an eighth sin. It is none of the Great Seven and an amalgam of all of them concurrently. It the sin of the gods. Self-Obsession.

Perhaps Lust should've known what she was getting herself into. But Lust when unleashed is a driving force of nature.

Perhaps Envy should've been stronger and should've said, Don't do this. But she was strangely Envious of the attention Lust was getting. She was used to getting that attention and sometimes even 'bad' or 'evil' attention is more appealing than no attention at all.

Perhaps Pride should've made some comment, any comment, should've offered assistance. Any word spoken could've changed the outcome of events. But being Prideful she thought she was above their petty lives.

Perhaps Sloth should've warned Lust that she was being given Doprinal but he lived his life to Not Give a Damn. He used all his personal resources to arrive at this point of Sloth.

Perhaps Anger should've run after Lust, her best friend, but Anger is fast and unrepentant.

Perhaps Avarice should've thought about the consequences of his actions but he wanted. Avarice is a slow drug.

Perhaps Gluttony should've sought psychological help for his transgressions but he was filled with the need with no room left for contrition.

Perhaps God should look on this world as if it were His first and as if all of the days were as the first day of Creation but He is Self-Obsessed.

Created in the image of God we are all Self-Obsessed and good, too good, at creating excuses. Our excuses are a miniature of that Seven Days of Genesis. A sin for every day.

So, what happened to Lust? She was gang-raped by ten men. Not many people could survive that. And what of the meek inheriting the earth? The meek have already got it. Now it's time to take it back.

The Contributors

KEVIN BROOKS was born in Exeter in 1959. He studied in Birmingham and London and now lives on the Essex/Suffolk border, writing full-time. His children's novel, *Martyn Pig*, will be published by the Chicken House in Spring 2002.

JENNIFER CLEMENT is the author of *The Next Stranger*, *Newton's Sailor*, *Widow Basquiat* (Payback Press, 2000) and *A True Story Based on Lies* (Canongate, 2001). She was part of the NYC art scene during the early Eighties and currently lives in Mexico City where she is the co-founder and director of the San Miguel Poetry Week.

NEIL COCKER was born in Falkirk in 1972. He works in the whisky industry. 'KGB Hairdressing' is an extract from *Sea of Tranquillity*, a novel in progress.

PAULO DA COSTA was born in Luanda, Angola and raised in the grape-growing lands of northern Portugal. He has lived in Alberta, Canada since 1989. He is the general editor of *Filling Station*, a Canadian literary magazine, and an associate editor of *OPIO Magazine* (Portugal).

LARI DON is thirty-two and lives in Edinburgh. She has been press officer for the Scottish National Party and a BBC radio producer. She is now a full-time mother. This is her first published work of fiction, because everything she wrote when she worked in politics was, of course, provable fact.

GARETH GOODALL was born in 1978 and found out about this win on his twenty-third birthday. He has lived in Bolton and then Uttoxeter before attending the University of Nottingham, graduating in 1999. He now lives in London working for an advertising agency. 'Salvage' is his first published piece of prose fiction.

ELAINE HOLOBOFF was born in Canada, and has lived in London for thirteen years. She has a D.Phil. from King's College London and numerous non-fiction publications. 'Second Coming' is her first prose publication. She has just completed her first novel, *Spirit Wrestlers*, and is moving to Hong Kong for several years to work on a second novel.

STEVE LEIGHTON was born in Exeter in 1952 and now lives in Glastonbury. He taught science for twenty years before taking early retirement to concentrate on writing, artwork and walking. 'By Weary Well' is his second published short story.

ADAM LLOYD-BAKER is the son of a Gloucestershire clergyman. He studied theology at Greenwich University. He has worked as a cathedral verger, a short-order cook in a New York diner, a gravedigger, a mortuary attendant and has fixed slot-machines in an Atlantic City casino. He currently works as a cinema projectionist in Cheltenham. His first novel *New York Graphic* ('A disturbing and dazzlingly assured achievement' – *The Observer*) is published by Gollancz.

ANDREW LLOYD-JONES was born in 1971 and grew up in Anchorage, Alaska. He studied English Literature at the University of York and is currently working in an advertising agency in central London. 'Coveting' is his first piece of published fiction.

HANNAH MCGILL was born in Shetland, grew up in Lincoln and went to Glasgow University. She now writes film reviews for *The Herald* and a weekly column for the *Sunday Times* 'Ecosse' section. Her short stories have appeared in *The Edinburgh Review* and the *Macallan/Scotland on Sunday Shorts* anthology.

JAN NATANSON lives in Kirriemuir. Her poetry appears in magazines and anthologies including *New Writing Scotland* and *Present Poets 2*. Short stories are published in *A Tongue in Yer Heid* (B&W Publishing) and *Mslexia* magazine. She mainly writes for theatre and is currently under commission to the Byre Theatre, St Andrews.

JOHN SAMSON was born and educated in Glasgow. He lives in Edinburgh where he teaches Chemistry. He is an occasional contributor to radio comedy scripts.

JANET FRANCES SMITH was born in the north of England and worked for more than twenty years as a journalist before turning to fiction. She has been working seriously on novels for children and writing adult short stories for light relief.

GEORGIA WILDER has been prolific and verbose since 1974. Georgia has self-published two books, *Prepping the Grinder* (Sydney, 1998) and *Bouncing the Network* (Belfast, 1999). She has also organised and participated in spoken word, open mic poetry and chaos-of-beat-and-words gigs on three continents.